THE TENSION WAS THICK ENOUGH
TO CUT WITH A KNIFE . . .

"Can you beat that, stranger?" the standing man with a bald head and jug-handle ears asked, his tone still gruff but his round and sweating face not expressing any desire one way or the other. Like the other three men who had decided to do more than simply leave it up to Red Wilmot to safeguard their investments in the game, he appeared totally indifferent to whether or not the stranger was proved to be a cheat by the arbitrary test set by the player with red hair.

Which probably meant, Steele suspected, that they intended to get back their money whatever kind of hand he had been dealt or had engineered for himself.

He took one gloved hand off the table. The right one. And scratched at his thigh.

"Well, Steele?" Wilmot demanded. "What you holdin', uh?"

The Virginian pursed his lips and raised one finger of his hand on the table to indicate the standing man with the gruff voice. "He never did count, because he wasn't in the game. Up until you turned over your cards, you could have paid to find out what I'm holding, feller. Way I've always played poker, you fellers have all folded, so the pot's mine."

He eased the left hand slowly forward to splay the fingers wide over the scattering of crumpled ones, fives and tens in the center of the table.

"No!" Wilmot roared and shot out his own left hand to slam it down hard over that of Steele. As he half rose from his chair and reached with his right hand under his left arm toward the small pile of cards in front of the Virginian.

Steele wanted to kill the man. . . .

THE ADAM STEELE SERIES:

#22

ADAM STEELE

THE BIG GAME

BY
George G. Gilman

PINNACLE BOOKS   NEW YORK

STEELE #22: THE BIG GAME

Copyright © 1979 by George G. Gilman

All rights reserved, including the right to reproduce this book or portions thereof in any form.

A Pinnacle Book. Originally published in 1979 in Great Britain by New English Library Ltd.

First printing, August 1982

ISBN: 0-523-41455-2

Cover illustration by George Bush

Printed in the United States of America

PINNACLE BOOKS, INC.
1430 Broadway
New York, New York 10018

For
Rose and Ron
who take care
of the animal

THE
BIG GAME

Chapter One

It was 9:30 at night, the rain had been stopped for at least two hours and Adam Steele was richer than he had been for a very long time. And he knew he had a good chance of more than doubling the two and a half thousand dollars, give or take a five spot, which was piled in an untidy heap on the green-baize-covered table in front of him. For he had just drawn two cards and against all the odds had filled a natural ace flush. And, as the three other players in the game drew either one or two cards, none showed any inclination to fold.

It had not started out to be a big game. Eight hours ago when the trio of men at a corner table in the Broken Promise Saloon asked the Virginian if he would care to take a hand in a friendly card school. And Steele had accepted

1

the invitation without making it known to the men that in his opinion there was no such animal as a friendly card school—when the game being played was poker.

It was an impulsive decision by the trail-wearied and travel-stained Virginian to nod in response to the question, turn away from the misused bar where he had finished drinking a cup of very bad coffee and go over to the only baize-draped table in the poorly-furnished saloon.

"Red Wilmot," the man with the deck in his hand introduced. "This here's John Tredeger and over there's Arnie Alton. Five card draw with deuces wild. Straight game with no fancy rules. Limit set by what's in a man's bankroll. We don't take no credit from a stranger and wouldn't expect you to take none from us."

It had been raining heavily on south Chicago then. Teeming out of a sky that was low and gray for as far as the eye could see in every direction.

The sky had been like that for a day and a half as Adam Steele rode slowly across the seemingly limitless prairie of northeastern Illinois. But the clouds did not unleash their threatened deluge until he was in off the tall grass plain and surrounded by the squat and ugly buildings of the city for which he had been heading for much longer than a day and a half.

He happened to be directly outside a saloon when the downpour began, on a length of street in a rundown commercial area that offered no other shelter. So it was that he hitched his black stallion to the rail under the jutting board sign reading BROKEN PROMISE, stepped across the sidewalk and pushed between the batwings into the long and narrow room with a bar along one of the short walls and sawdust-strewn floor scattered with a dozen tables encircled by mismatched chairs.

Wilmot, Tredeger and Alton were the only other customers and there was just the one elderly bartender—who grimaced when Steele asked for coffee, but supplied it from out back for the same price as beer.

The rain drummed on the flat roof of the single-story, frame-built saloon and rattled at the loose-fitting windows to either side of the entrance. The three middle-aged men at the corner table played an unexciting game of penny-ante poker, calling softly and chinking the coins quietly in front of them. The bartender, having served the coffee and accepted payment for it, resumed his previous pastime of staring vacantly into space and clicking his false dentures together in his slack jaw.

Steele found himself thinking that if this place was representative of the city of Chicago, it was well named. As he took the final swig of weak coffee. At which point Red Wilmot made him the offer to join the game and, after checking that the rain was showing no sign of letting up, he went over to take the fourth chair at the table.

The three men, who were all between fifty and sixty, were dressed in denim work clothes

3

but their shirts and pants and boots were as clean as their hands and face. And as hard-used but as well-preserved. So Steele judged them, on first impression, to be manual workers who were now either retired or laid-off. Killing time with small stakes card games while they made their glasses of beer last for as long as possible in the Broken Promise. But the Virginian had lived too long on the dangerous side of life to trust first impressions. He was therefore prepared to alter his assessment if the rain kept up and the game lasted any length of time.

When he was twenty-five dollars ahead, he asked the bartender to have the stallion taken to the closest livery stable and the loose-jawed man with the noisy false teeth called out a negro youth to do this. Without scowling. And he did not even show any bad grace when Steele asked for another cup of coffee—adding that he would be grateful if this time it was fresh made.

For the game was getting interesting. To him as a spectator as well as to all four of the players. On the surface it was still friendly: the players making easy-going conversation and keeping their stakes low. But the pennies, nickels, dimes and quarters had been picked off the table by now, to be replaced by silver and paper dollars. Four fives and two tens as well.

"You got business in the city, Mr. Steele?" Wilmot asked as he and the Virginian watched Tredeger and Alton try to out-bluff each other.

"No."

"Beg your pardon. Didn't mean to pry."

Steele shook his head. "Forget it, you're not.

Guess you could say I'm a sightseer. I've never been to Chicago before. And it happened to be at the end of the trail I was riding."

Wilmot looked pleased. For this was the most he or the other had been able to get the stranger to say all at one time. "Much like any other city, I guess. In the north, leastways. You're from a southern city, I'd say. By the way you talk and the cut of your clothes?"

"From outside a small town in Virginia, a long time ago," Steele supplied as Tredeger called and his two pair were no match for Alton's three of a kind.

Actually, he came from a long way outside of that small town, for his father's plantation was one of the largest in the state. Before and during the Civil War. But now the Steele Plantation, like the man who had created it, was no more. And it was the war—and Ben Steele's allegiance to the north while his son elected to ride as a Confederate cavalry lieutenant—which had set this man out on the trail which brought him to the Broken Promise Saloon on the south side of Chicago this rain-drenched Saturday. With, resting against his chair as he played a game of friendly poker, a Colt Hartford revolving rifle with a fire-scorched rosewood stock to which was screwed a gold plate inscribed: TO BENJAMIN P. STEELE, WITH GRATITUDE—ABRAHAM LINCOLN.

They had all noticed how he carried the unusual rifle into the Broken Promise with him, kept it within reach of his right hand while he stood at the bar and then ensured it was easily accessible when he took the chair at the table. Which was explained, up to a point, when he took off his wet topcoat and draped it over a nearby chair to dry. For he did not carry a conventional handgun in a visible holster. Like so many of the strangers who provided the saloon's passing trade: cow punchers, most of them, dressed western style complete with a Colt slung in a low holster hanging from one side of a gunbelt.

This stranger was not like that at all. He was dressed like a dude who had been down on his luck for a long time. In a well-cut and expensive once-pale-blue city suit which was now heavily soiled. Beneath this was a purple vest with some of its buttons missing and a lace-trimmed white shirt which was both soiled and torn. A string necktie was neatly knotted between the points of the shirt collar. Also around his neck, but hanging outside the lapels of his suit jacket was a gray silk kerchief. On his head was a low crowned, wide-brimmed black Stetson and on his feet he wore black riding boots, spurless and with his pants cuffs outside. His topcoat was high collared and reached to below his knees and it could be buttoned from throat to hem.

So, a down-at-heel citified dude who had been attired, also, for facing whatever the elements chose to hurl at him while he was riding across the big country towards Chicago.

A slightly built dude, but by no means a puny one. He was no more than a half inch over five and a half feet tall but there was more than a mere hint of lean strength in his bearing.

6

He was in his late thirties, but could look several years younger when he spread a somewhat boyish smile across his deeply bronzed, heavily lined, nondescriptly handsome face: this expression tending to cancel out the aging effect of his prematurely gray hair which he wore trimmed short. His eyes were coal black, his mouthline was gentle and his jaw had a resolute set.

At first glance, he looked like an easy-to-get-along-with guy, short of money but familiar with such a situation and unconcerned by it. Only when it was noticed that the rifle was almost an extension of the man and that the hands which were never far from the gun were tightly encased in black buckskin gloves— gunslinger style in the view of the other men in the Broken Promise—was it possible to guess that Adam Steele was not what he appeared on the surface to be. Which was the kind of man who could use the Colt Hartford with great skill and speed. The kind who carried a throwing knife in a boot sheath, the weapon accessible through a split in the outside seam of his right pants leg. The kind who wore, for a kerchief, an oriental weapon of strangulation—a thuggee's scarf with carefully balanced weights sewn into diagonally opposite corners.

"Weren't aimin' to be nosy at all, Mr. Steele," Wilmot hurried on after Alton had clawed in his winnings and Tredeger began a new deal. "Not for the sake of it, anyways. But seein' as how John and Arnie and me know a lot of folks

7

in this city, I was just wonderin' if we could've helped you."

"Grateful to you. Just sightseeing, is all." And forgetting—but that was his business—how he had used Sara to get over Renita and found himself stuck with hard-to-unload memories of both of them.

"Two cards," Red Wilmot said.

"I'll stay with these," Steele told John Trede-ger, and ensured without making it obvious, that the teeth-clicking bartender could not see the full-house queens and sevens which was his pat hand.

It was good enough to win, but the pot was low. The hand taught him a little more about the other players, though. Knowledge which in the game of poker was almost as important to have as good cards.

During the early years, up until the start of the War Between the States, Adam Steele's life had been little more than a series of pleasant games, with the decks always stacked by his father's wealth to ensure that he came out the winner. But the war changed all that, as it did for tens of thousands of other young men. When skills he had acquired in sport—riding, hunting and shooting—had to be developed and honed so that he was better able to find and kill the Union enemy. The slaughter justifiable because if you didn't kill them, they would kill you.

Then the war ended and the younger Steele rode eagerly towards a meeting with his father, both men prepared to forget their differences of the past and pick up the threads of the fine life which had been severed by the opening shots of war. Adam Steele anxious to forget, also, how when there was a cause for which to fight and a uniform to protect you from legal retribution, the hunting down and killing of men could be great sport.

Far more exciting than poker.

All through the afternoon and into the early evening the rain continued to fall. Not so heavily as when the downpour began, but hard and fast enough to make even the squalid shelter of the Broken Promise Saloon seem like the height of luxury when compared with the prospect of riding the muddy streets through the needling raindrops.

The Virginian had just used his gloved hands to draw in another fifty-dollar pot when he glanced out under the batwings and had this thought. But then, as Arnie Alton dealt the cards for another hand, he glanced around the saloon and corrected the rather ill-founded opinion. The saloon itself was merely a conveniently located roof and four walls into which a man with any sense could come to get out of the rain. No better and no worse than a great many other similar establishments he had visited on the long and tortuous trail he had ridden between Washington and Chicago.

Why he felt so comfortable here was accountable in part to the company and in part to the poker game.

Throughout the afternoon the game continued as quietly as it began and Steele was pre-

9

pared to admit that his first impression of the other players had been correct and that his later suspicions about them—and the bartender—were groundless. For the stakes remained relatively low as good fortune was shared equally among all the players. Wilmot, Tredeger and Alton chatted and joked among themselves, with Steele and with other men who entered and left the Broken Promise.

By the time it had got dark enough for the bartender to touch a taper to the half dozen kerosene lamps which lit the place, the four players were all about back where they started. And Steele was struck by the thought that he was involved in something he had once considered impossible: a friendly poker game. A gentle diversion to kill time until the weather cleared up. Sharing a few pleasant hours with some men who had days and weeks and months to use up—for it had emerged in the talk that the trio were, indeed, former stockyard workers whose strengths and skills were no longer required.

"Well, boys," John Tredeger said with a quiet smile as he fanned open his cards after drawing one. "I reckon I got good enough here to make it worthwhile stakin' a little more than I usually put up. Twenty bucks to stay all right with you gentlemen?"

He had opened for a dollar.

Now he looked at his buddies first and then at Steele, his sparse eyebrows arched in a manner which expressed it was a question he was

10

willing to have answered in the negative and not be offended.

"Said at the outset the limit was a man's bankroll," Red Wilmot reminded, addressing himself primarily to the Virginian.

Who nodded his agreement with the red-headed man and his willingness to play the kind of game the hollow-cheeked Tredeger was suggesting.

Arnie Alton sighed.

And so did Steele, as he shot a glance towards the bartender and caught the man displaying his noisy false teeth in an avaricious smile. In contrast to Alton's sigh, Steele's was inward and silent: a secret expression of mixed emotions. Of mild sadness that he had been right to distrust these men who were only pretending to be friendly towards him: and of pleasure that the game was going to develop into the kind of poker he most enjoyed playing. The kind with no quarter asked nor given. With the added spice, on this occasion, of knowing that the other three players considered him a rich sucker ready to be taken.

"You'll also recall, Mr. Steele," Wilmot added, "that in this school no credit is given. It's cash on the line or—"

"I have a good memory, feller," the Virginian cut in.

Wilmot nodded and grinned. "I hope you have cards to match it, sir."

"Hey, not too good!" Tredeger said quickly and laughed.

11

Steele's lips curled away from his white teeth and to the men at the table he seemed to be expressing the boyish smile which he had showed so often during the afternoon. But, because of the shadow thrown over his upper face by his hat brim, they did not see that his eyes were impassive—like black and shiny pebbles.

"That's for me to know and you fellers to find out," he said lightly, without anyone being aware that the lack of feeling in his eyes totally cancelled out any meaning which his tone of voice might suggest.

"I'm in," Wilmot said, placing his twenty dollars in the center of the table, his smile becoming self-satisfied.

"Me, too," Alton announced and swelled the pot by a like amount. He could not resist a surreptitious glance to Steele.

"I'm out," Steele drawled, and as he folded four tens he looked quickly and secretly at each man: seeking in their eyes confirmation that he was right—or a clue that he was wrong.

But none of them expressed any kind of surprise or disappointment. And there was no way of knowing the value of the hand which Alton folded before Wilmot asked Tredeger to show and the opener's aces and kings full house took the pot.

"You gotta speculate to accumulate, ain't that what they say, Mr. Steele?" the hollow-cheeked man posed gleefully as he stacked his winnings in front of him.

"What people say and what they do can be two different things, feller," the Virginian growled, and just for a moment allowed his icy calmness to falter: to show them, if the men had the sensitivity to realize it, that deep down he would have preferred the game to have remained on a friendly basis. "Depending upon whether or not they get a good deal."

Chapter Two

There had been moments—perhaps enough moments to stretch to periods—in Adam Steele's relatively recent past when he had indulged in the self-pity of claiming, to himself, that life had given him a bad deal. But no more. For he had learned, as most men learned much earlier, that they had to play the cards life dealt them. Either that or cry—maybe even perish—in the wilderness.

The trail which had begun in Washington and brought him to Chicago had started, in more precise terms, in a bar-room across the street from Ford's Theater on the night that Abraham Lincoln was assassinated. For on that same misty April night in the year 1865 another man had died. Benjamin P. Steele, lynched from a beam in that bar-room on Tenth Street.

As he played cards in another bar-room, half a country and many years away from that one where he had been scheduled to meet his father and take the first steps towards forgetting the past, Adam Steele could view the events of that night and the countless days and nights which followed dispassionately.

A group of rebels and assassins had hanged his father wantonly and uselessly, to divert attention from what was about to happen across the street in Ford's Theater. But the wider implications of the killing had not occurred to Adam Steele—and if they had they would certainly have not affected his actions at the time.

That night of 14 April 1865, he fired the first shot of what was to be the violent peace following a bloody war. For a single life for a single life was not enough. Everyone responsible for the lynching of Ben Steele had to die before Adam Steele could feel that his thirst for vengeance had been slaked. For these people had to pay also—Steele was now, dispassionately, able to acknowledge—for the destruction of the plantation and the big house. Laid waste not by the lynchers, but by a nameless and faceless mob of southern sympathizers who were not as prepared as his son to forgive Ben Steele's sin of supporting the Union against the Confederacy.

How much the murder of his father and how much the loss of his birthright . . . ? Which wanton act had been the major driving force behind Adam Steele's murderous ride into the west? Always he had considered the isolated incident of Ben Steele's violent demise as the sole

reason for the mass slaughter he committed—
that burst of wholesale killing in which his own
best friend had died. For Steele had neither a
patriotic cause nor a uniform to justify his act
of vengeance and so the law demanded he be
called to answer for what he had done.

And the officer of the law they sent to get
him was Jim Bishop, his boyhood pal. Who
made the mistake of trusting an old friend.

"Mr. Steele," John Tredeger rasped as he
mopped beads of perspiration from his shiny
high forehead, "you sure are one lucky card
player."

The unsweating, impassive-faced Virginian
added the eighty-six-dollar pot to the sprawling
heap of silver and paper money in front of him
and shook his head. "Wrong, feller," he drawled.
"The name of this card game is poker and luck
has nothing to do with it."

"Surely, sir, a man has to have the luck to be
dealt the cards?" a man asked.

It was now pitch dark outside. The rain had
ceased to fall but the cloud cover was still solid,
despite a powerful wind that was blowing angrily from out of the north. A norther coming in
cold and hard enough to cause the bartender to
close the outer doors in front of the batwings.

As he played cards, concentrating almost ex-
clusively on the game, Steele was aware of
these outer doors opening and closing. To admit new customers—never to let anyone out.
Each time a draft curled into the Broken Promise, to set the kerosene lamps swaying or flicker-
ing and to chill the stove warmed air, he briefly

17

glanced away from the faces of the men with whom he was playing. To look with apparent nonchalance at the faces of the new-comers. A glance was always enough. For he never recognized anyone from his past and none of the strangers ever returned his passing attention with more than mild curiosity.

Many of those who came in out of the windy night he had seen earlier in the day: obviously employees in the nearby warehouses who used the Broken Promise during work-breaks and also after they had finished for the day. Others were total strangers to Steele but were known to Wilmot, Tredeger and Alton. With the exception of two men, one of whom directed the question at the Virginian.

"If you don't get the cards, feller," Steele replied, "you fold the hand and wait until you get something you can bet with."

The two men were different from all the others—whether watching the game or simply drinking and totally ignoring it—in other ways than simply not being known to either Steele's card playing companions or the bartender.

They were in a younger age group—between twenty-five and thirty whereas everyone else in the Broken Promise was close to forty or well beyond that age. Also, this pair had quite obviously never had to do any manual outside labor in their lives—for they had the soft hands and pale complexions of men who worked inside, or did not work at all. And, in contrast to the hard-wearing and rough-cut clothing of the other patrons, these men were dressed city-style in suits which—Steele's expert eye judged—had been made by the finest tailor in Chicago.

"Hey, Steele," Red Wilmot muttered with irritation in his voice. "You sure you ain't a professional poker player?"

"I'm still sure, feller," the Virginian answered evenly as he shuffled and then started to deal the cards. "You asked me that already, and I told you. A liar I'm not."

Except to himself, perhaps. If that was possible. For surely a man could not—for any length of time—deceive himself?

After he killed Bish, Steele rode aimlessly and found himself in Mexico. In a small village where he tried to drown in hard liquor an emotion he had never experienced before. Remorse.

He could have died in that village of Nuevo Rio. From the effects of drinking too much, sure. But he stopped before that happened. Also, from a bullet in the heart or a slit throat. But he was lucky because they were good people at the cantina where he went through his drinking jag. Far too good to take advantage of a *loco Americano*.

How many good people had he met since he rode away from Nuevo Rio, that tiny village which was probably as important in his life as Washington in terms of a point on the trail which had brought him to the Broken Promise Saloon on the south side of Chicago? Probably more good than bad. But he was seldom in the right frame of mind to differentiate between the two. And it seemed that whenever he was, the people he chose to judge turned out to be on the wrong side of the line.

Like today.

"Fifty dollars," Arnie Alton said and smacked his thin lips together as he accompanied the words with the act and dropped the bills into the pot.

"Stay," the Virginian added, placing his ace-flush natural face down on the table in a neat five-card stack before he covered the bet.

All three of the other players could not conceal their feelings about Steele's decision to play his hand. And, if he had allowed himself the luxury, he knew he could have easily felt sympathy for the men. Because this was a straight game. Earlier he had been doubtful about this. But now he was certain. The cards were not marked and they all came off the top of the deck. So all that was wrong with the game was that Wilmot, Tredeger and Alton were playing as a team against him. But there was nothing crooked in that. Not to Steele's mind.

They were three out-of-work and hard-up men, not yet old enough to be tossed on life's scrapheap. Who attempted to raise a little extra cash—whether for the needs of their families or to buy beer he had no way of knowing—by taking any eager poker-playing passing stranger to the cleaners. Backed when necessary, it appeared from his keen interest in the way the game was going, by the bartender of the Broken Promise.

And when they tried they were good at what they did. Bad at bluffing, but better than the average poker hustlers who haunted saloons like this one in small trail towns or on the fringes of big cities. Probably they made quite a few small killings with cowpunchers, itinerant stockyard and cannery workers and railroadmen who would compromise most of the strangers in this part of Chicago. Men who thought that winning and losing at poker had something to do with luck.

For five hands now, the Broken Promise Saloon had been tensely silent as everyone concentrated upon the game being played at the corner table. For all of the men in the smoke-filled, liquor-smelling, stove-heated room—with two exceptions—had a financial interest in the outcome. Because the rule concerning credit applied only between the players themselves. Hard-cash money could be borrowed from beyond the table and Wilmot, Tredeger and Alton had all borrowed heavily. From the bartender at first but then, after the man with the noisy teeth had said no more, from the customers. And the money was given readily, by men who were obviously used to seeing the players they staked come out on top at the end of the game.

Until that moment when Adam Steele covered Arnie Alton's ante and the three local players were unable to conceal that this disconcerted them. For then the silence, which had always held a quality of high excitement and keen anticipation of victory, abruptly became uneasy. As, whether by instinct or from experience, the gallery of watchers realized the crisis point had been reached. When the stranger, having been set up, was now to be taken.

"I'll stay, too," Tredeger said huskily, after looking at Wilmot as if for encouragement and getting no response at all.

"I need a couple of hundred bucks," the redheaded man growled. His cards were face down on the table, still in a fan. Which gave him both hands free to thrust out to the sides, palms uppermost.

"Where would we get that kinda cash, Red?" a bearded oldtimer asked bitterly.

Wilmot tried to look into Steele's pebble-like eyes in the shadow of the hat brim and failed. "Look," he countered and stared into the shaded area anyway. "If you guys want to get your money back and more, you'll raise the money. Between you. Go home and get it if you have to. I just know I've got the beatin' of Steele."

He was angry. Perhaps humiliated, too. The top man of the trio who therefore carried the responsibility for asking the stranger to play cards and then taking all this time to get him to a point of no return—which turned out to be not for Steele at all. So Red Wilmot had made a bad misjudgment.

"You mind waitin' awhile if we have to?" the man asked, looking suddenly much older than his age: as if the strain of attempting to maintain his composure under pressure was a great drain on his physical stamina as well as his strength of mind.

"You made the rule, feller," Steele replied evenly, and discovered he was prepared to give a break to the players and to their backers. To cut their losses rather than to increase them. "No credit. Let you bend that rule a little. No more. Rain's stopped and I can be on my way."

"Damn it, mister, you gotta give us a chance to get our money back!" Arnie Alton snarled.

"Yeah, you gotta have taken us for better than two grand of hard-earned money, Steele!" John Tredeger snapped. "It ain't right you should just get up from the table and walk outta here with—"

"As I recall, there wasn't any rule made about when the game was scheduled to end," the Virginian put in. And allowed his gaze to wander away from his fellow players and briefly survey the faces of the watchers who stood in a close-packed half circle around one side of the table. "My stomach says it's time."

The two fancy dressers who were the last men to join the audience—they had not even got wet—returned his attention with open curiosity, the taller one with the mean-looking eyes showing the start of a sneer of scorn in the way he set his lips to sip at a glass of beer.

The bartender felt no need to conceal his anger and he glowered at all the players, not differentiating between the men he had staked and the man who had won his money from them.

The remainder of the watchers—about twenty or so—were for the most part nervously eager for the situation to be resolved. One way or the other. Four men, as contemptuous of Wolmot, Tredeger and Alton as the mean-eyed dude was of Steele, began to ease their way to the front of the semi-circle of men.

"For some reason this guy's being easy on you people," the shorter, thicker-set and less demonstrative dude said evenly, he and his partner as aware as Steele of the four men who were closing in. "He figures he has the beating of you and he's giving you a chance to quit and call it a day."

"Who asked you to poke in your nose, mister?" Wilmot growled and shifted his angry and worried gaze to the unmoving, thickly bristled face of the Virginian. "You know him, Steele?"

"No, feller. How about you and these four?"

The grim-faced quartet with sneers twisting their mouths, had reached the front of the curved line. They were all in their mid-forties, built for heavy work and still smeared with the dirt and stale with the sweat from a long day of earning money the hard way.

Wilmot was suddenly more composed. He had not seen the men make their move until they emerged at the front of the group. When he looked at them fearfully, received a nod of encouragement from one of them and immediately felt better.

"Only three people in this saloon I don't know, Steele," he replied confidently. "On account of this is my neck of the woods and it's a real friendly place. To live in."

"Where strangers are welcome, so long as

they don't have winning ways?" Steele asked evenly.

"We don't want no trouble," Tredeger said, and tried to swallow the nervousness which had risen into his throat and stuck there, like a piece of food he had not chewed enough.

"Damn right!" the bartender added and his voice had a quiver in it. "Not in my saloon."

The majority of the audience shuffled backwards from the card table, scraping chair-legs on the sawdust-strewn floor as they bumped into furniture in their haste. A glass crashed to the floor and a man cursed.

"Oh, no," the bartender moaned. "Can't you settle this outside on the street?"

Steele and Alton sat with their backs to the wall and so were best placed to see how the backing off of most of the watchers had left the two well-dressed strangers and the four toughest looking local men in an untidy semicircle behind Wilmot and Tredeger. The redheaded man and his hollow-cheeked partner had glanced quickly to the side to see if the sounds of movement meant what they thought, and now Tredeger was as composed as Wilmot: both of them apparently unworried by the presence of the young dudes.

The Virginian pursed his lips in the line of a sigh but made no sound. As he saw a tacit message flash between the eyes of Alton and Wilmot. The latter gave an almost imperceptible nod of acknowledgement, then gave away the secret by glancing at the Colt Hartford and moving his booted foot an inch in the direction of where the stock rested on the floor.

More trouble. Coming from out of nowhere, uninvited.

When he had discovered the corpse of his father swinging from a lynch rope in the Washington bar-room, Steele had certainly done all he could to seek trouble. Both before and after he buried the remains on the ruined plantation and took possession of the only material bequest he was to receive from Ben Steele—the Colt Hartford five-shot sporting rifle with a revolving action. For trouble of the worst kind was what a man invited when he rode a violent trail through a post-war peace to find and kill men who should have been left for the law to deal with.

After he did what he had to do? And after he lost his taste for liquor while trying to submerge remorse in it? Well, sometimes he went looking for trouble again. Because he had to earn money to feed and clothe himself and to keep a horse that he could ride from one point on his trail to the next. And, because of the kind of man he had become—the kind people of perception recognized him to be—the work he got was often of the troublesome sort.

When it was not, or when he was not even working, the threat of violence seldom retreated far from wherever he happened to be. It was his fate to be trailed by such a threat or to have it lying in wait for him around a curve on the way he was headed. A fate, he sometimes felt, which was destiny's method of punishing him in the stead of the due process of law he escaped after his vengeance killings of his father's lynchers and his cold-blooded murder of Jim Bishop.

But recently, after another ride into Mexico—his second since the drinking jag in Nuevo Rio—he had started to distrust the abstract concept of some supernatural being guiding his own steps and those of potential enemies on to the same course.

It had been his own decision to involve himself with the troubles of young Jimmy Dexter which resulted in the two of them having to travel another stretch of violent trail. And there had been no invisible guiding hand reaching down out of the sky to hold him in Sun City until the simmering trouble boiled over to spill hot blood rather than hot water. San Francisco and Renita and the bunch of political fanatics who tried to force him to commit murder? Maybe he could blame a twist of fate for involving him in that outburst of slaughter. But after he was involved, he could have disentangled himself, if he had chosen to ignore his feelings for the Mexican woman. While the kids on the eastward bound wagon train . . . He had to accept full responsibility for electing to take a share in the mess they had brought upon themselves. Because of a woman again. No, not even a woman. A girl.

Invariably there was an easily identifiable reason for doing what he did: to enmesh himself in the problems of other people which almost always resulted in him being the prime mover in solving these problems. By using his rifle, throwing knife, thuggee's scarf or some other weapon against his fellow human beings.

But since this latest ride into Mexico, which he had undertaken in a subconscious effort to backtrack on his life and try to pick up one of the many broken threads, he had gradually come to acknowledge that such reasons as he could freely pinpoint were surface excuses for his underlying, deep-seated motivation.

"Turn over them cards, Steele," Red Wilmot said icily. "Your luck's just too good to be true."

"You want to come right out and say what you mean, feller?" the Virginian answered, not moving his body and limbs: sitting absolutely still on the chair with his gloved hands resting palms down to either side of his money and the five neatly stacked pasteboards.

"If you got the beatin' of us, seems to me there ain't no other explanation except that you're a cheatin' sonofabitch!"

Wilmot's voice was soft-spoken until he reached the final words. And these he spat out forcefully, along with some droplets of saliva. As he lashed forward his left foot and made contact with the stock of the rifle.

The spittle sprayed the table and made wet marks on the green baize. The Colt Hartford fell to the floor with a crash which the sparse scattering of sawdust did little to mute.

"Oh, Jesus," the bartender rasped, and almost lost his dentures.

At the same time Tredeger and Alton gasped their shock at Wilmot's dangerous voicing of the accusation. And at the Virginian's apparent stoic acceptance of it.

"Red, that's a little . . ." Tredeger began.

"The man plays a better game than you people, that's all," the shorter of the two fancy dressers said evenly, as he eyed the unmoving and silent Steele with mild apprehension.

His companion's scorn deepened and he looked as if he felt like spitting.

"Hey, all I got is two pair, aces and queens," Arnie Alton said hoarsely, and tossed his cards face up on the table.

"Mine's a full house," Tredeger added hurriedly, and fumbled with shaking hands to turn over his cards and display the three tens and two aces.

"What you got, Red?" the spokesman for the local players' quartet of back-up men asked gruffly.

"Me?" He turned over his cards one at a time, gaining confidence with each flick of the fingers that sent the pasteboards to the table. Four low clubs and the deuce of spades. "Twos are wild, so I reckon I got me an ace flush." He stared hard into the shadowed area beneath Steele's hat brim, deciding he had a fix on the dark eyes he could not see. As he parted his lips to show a thin grin of expected triumph—which meant, the Virginian knew, that Red Wilmot expected his flush with a wild card to be a loser.

"Can you beat that, stranger?" the standing man with a bald head and jug-handle ears asked, his tone still gruff but his round and sweating face not expressing any desire one way or the other. Like the other three men who had decided to do more than simply leave it up to Red Wilmot to safeguard their investments in the game, he appeared totally indifferent to whether or not the stranger was proved to be a cheat by the arbitrary test set by the player with red hair.

Which probably meant, Steele suspected, that they intended to get back their money whatever kind of hand he had been dealt or had engineered for himself.

He took one gloved hand off the table. The right one. And scratched at his thigh.

"Well, Steele?" Wilmot demanded. "What you holdin', uh?"

The Virginian pursed his lips and raised one finger of his hand on the table to indicate the standing man with the gruff voice. "He never did count, because he wasn't in the game. Up until you turned over your cards, you could have paid to find out what I'm holding, feller. Way I've always played poker, you fellers have all folded, so the pot's mine."

He eased the left hand slowly forward to splay the fingers wide over the scattering of crumpled ones, fives and tens in the center of the table.

"No!" Wilmot roared and shot out his own left hand to slam it down hard over that of Steele. As he half rose from his chair and reached with his right hand under his left arm toward the small pile of cards in front of the Virginian.

Steele wanted to kill the man. Arnie Alton,

30

too. And John Tredeger. The bartender with the loose and noisy false teeth. The four men who were ready and willing to show how tough they were. All the others who had put up money in confident expectation—based on experience?—that they would get it back, plus interest. Maybe, too, the tall, broad-shouldered dude in the well-cut suit and topcoat who from the expression on his freshly shaven and talced face also thought the Virginian a fool. Even the man who had come into the Broken Promise with the one who harbored so much contempt. For he looked as if it would take very little more to convince him that he should share his partner's opinion.

Many years ago, before the war and during most of it, in a situation such as this, Adam Steele might have done just that. Killed, or attempted to kill, everyone who had set him up, falsely accused him, or simply looked at him with scorn while they underestimated his ability to respond to detractors. For one of his major character faults as a youth and young man had been his quick and almost uncontrollable temper.

This tendency to erupt into a furious rage, given what he considered a just cause to do so, was innate and because of his privileged and rather spoiled childhood he had little need to try to exercise self-control. And for much of the war it acted to his advantage, often proving as useful in killing the enemy as his skill as a horseman and with a rifle and saber. But then fortune took a twist and an incident occurred which set him on the path to learning how to curb the vindictive rages which had cost him so many friends—and the Union so many lives—since he was old enough to demand and get what he wanted.

Since that incident in the distant past far to the east and south of Chicago, Adam Steele had invariably been able to control his emotions whatever they were: to the extent that some people who had known him were convinced the Virginian never had any feelings about anything or anybody. An exception to this, of course, had been during the period between finding his father's body hanging from a beam and strangling the life's breath out of Bish.

Was that a single exception? He could think of no others. Unless he counted every other victim who had died, violently, by his hand. Killed not for those facile reasons he could pluck out of thin air to justify to himself and to others why he squeezed the trigger, threw the knife or jerked his hands apart with the thuggee's scarf fisted in them. Instead, struck down out of well-concealed temper. By a man filled with vicious resentments rooted way back in the mid-April of the year 1865. When it had been relatively easy to identify, track down and punish the men who lynched his father. While those who set fire to the plantation fields and put a torch to the big house were allowed to escape unscathed.

Was that why Adam Steele rode an endless and aimless trail, looking for excuses to kill?

Deluding himself with rational reasons to explain his acts of violence. While all the time the truth was buried deep in his subconscious, waiting for him to uncover it. That, denied the opportunity to punish the culprits who had done more to rob him of his birthright than the lynchers of his father, he had chosen to lash out indiscriminately at anyone who was unfortunate enough to cross him. Like a bad-tempered and spoiled child. But not a child anymore. A man. And a man who knew more ways to kill than most.

Worse than this, even. A man with a seemingly insatiable lust to strike back for what he had lost. Who, when trouble did not come to him, went looking for it. As on this wet Saturday on the south side of Chicago when he had, without encouraging this ugly situation to develop, done nothing to prevent it.

Steele's right hand came up above the level of the table, a split second after the shoulder had dipped for an instant to lengthen his reach. Everyone except the two dudes instinctively leaned backwards, aware from the speed of the move that the Virginian was in the process of a counter to Wilmot's action. And all expected him to bring up the rifle which had been kicked to the floor on that side of his chair.

But the shoulder didn't dip low enough for Steele to curl his hand around the frame of the Colt Hartford. And what he was grasping was seen as little more than a blurred flash of glinting metal as his fisted hand rose and then was hurled down—to smash, end-on into the back of Wilmot's hand a moment before the fingertips of the red-haired man could touch the cards.

Wilmot's scream was piercingly shrill. And for part of a second as all eyes swung to stare into his pain-contorted face, there was curiosity expressed at why a grown man would respond with such a high-pitched and agonized sound to a mere blow.

But then they saw the blood stain expanding darkly across the green baize to either side of the flat hand with the fisted one on top of it. Saw, also, the handle of a knife protruding from the top of the gloved fist of Steele. And realized that the knife had been plunged through the hand and then through the table, pinning one to the other: the initial slight pain of the honed blade stabbing into flesh expanded to intense agony as Wilmot instinctively attempted to withdraw his hand and the metal tore at his sinews.

"Dear God in heaven!" Alton gasped, and knocked over his chair and almost stumbled to the floor himself as he sought to escape from the table: put to flight by Steele's action of reaching down, scooping up the rifle and cocking the hammer.

Wilmot's scream was curtailed by the merciful release of a faint. As Steele stood up, pressed the muzzle of the rifle into the forearm of the red-headed man, and jerked the knife blade out of the table and the hand. The metal made a small sucking sound as it came clear of the flesh, and the blood flowed freely, brightly crimson, from the elongated wound. Thus freed from constraint, the weight of Wilmot's unfeeling torso dragged his arms off the table and he tipped to the side and became heaped on the floor.

Steele was now the unopposed center of attention, as he rested his right foot on his chair to push the blood-stained knife back through the slit in his pants leg and into the boot sheath. At the same time he canted the still-cocked rifle to his shoulder. All the while raking his eyes from left to right and back again—checking on the faces and hands of the shocked, and in two cases, admiring—men who gazed at him.

He thought that the two men in the stylish clothes who were impressed by his moves had guns. And that the bartender probably had a revolver or shotgun under the counter. But none of these made a move to get the drop on the Virginian. While the rest of the men in the Broken Promise would be armed only with knives, if they were armed at all.

The four men who had a few moments before been prepared to supply the muscle to back Red Wilmot's play had now faded into the larger group. Arnie Alton had gone with them. Which left just John Tredeger and the two dudes in isolation before Steele as he began, one-handed, to gather up his money—including the pot—and stuff it into the side pocket of his suit jacket. His actions were deliberate and unhurried.

"You play a mean game of poker, Mr. Steele," the taller of the two dudes said.

"Just play the cards I'm dealt and draw, feller," he replied, and interrupted his collection of the bills to pick up the five pasteboards from in front of his former chair and slide them into the center of the pack. "As any man who cares to pay can see."

"Even if we'd seen what you held, mister, we wouldn't have known for sure if you was cheatin' or not, would we?" John Tredeger posed, staring morosely at the ugly stains on the green baize where Wilmot had bled.

"Help any, feller, I'll tell you this," the Virginian said at length after he had picked up the last of the bills. "Poker or the other game your partner was playing, he had a bad hand."

Chapter Three

There were glares of hatred and rasping sounds of resentful animosity as the Virginian went to the door of the Broken Promise Saloon. While John Tredeger crouched to check on Red Wilmot's condition and everyone else looked toward the slow-moving man who was responsible for the wounding.

He seemed to be carrying the Colt Hartford in one hand as casually as he held the topcoat in the other. And his dark eyes, which now could be sometimes glimpsed as he moved out of one area of brightest lamp light into another, were a perfect match for the neutral expression which had spread across his other features after he callously wrenched the knife from Wilmot's flesh. But everyone in the bar-room had a recent vivid recollection of how the short of stature but compactly strong man had exploded from apparant inoffensive nonchalance into vicious action. And so, without the weapons or skills to match those of the stranger, the regular patrons of the Broken Promise confined the releasing of their antagonisms to soft-spoken words and surreptitious glowers.

Steele could almost feel the massed emotions as a palpable force pressing against him while he moved among the tables to get to the doorway. But he paid scant attention to the men, for he could sense the frustration which told of their helplessness.

And he spared just one brief glance back into the hot and smoky, malodorous, hate-filled saloon before he pushed the outer doors closed. To check that the two dudes were still showing as much interest in him as when they had watched the poker game. Then, breathing deeply of the cool, damp night air, he moved along the sidewalk, through the patch of light from the misted window of the saloon and into the near pitch darkness beyond.

He felt good as he stepped down off the end of the sidewalk and moved through the mud of the street across the fronts of warehouses and factories toward a lamplit sign above the doorway of a livery stable. A lot easier in his mind than when he had ridden in off the prairie just before the start of the rainstorm. And not just because he had won a healthy bankroll and in the process had shown a bunch of city-slickers how wrong they had been to think of him as an easy mark.

No, his peace of mind came from the self knowledge he had finally admitted to himself. Which meant that he was the master of his own future. His own man. Without need to excuse himself to himself. Still filled with bitterness at losing what he considered as a right to be his. And making the wrong people pay. But not innocent people—as might have been the case if he had not learned how to control his temper. No, those who suffered or died at his hand may have had nothing whatever to do with robbing him of his birthright: but one way or another they sought to prevent him getting it back.

Steele knew he was being followed as he moved without haste along the dark street toward the stable with the dimly lit sign hanging above its doorway. But he knew who the men behind him were—had seen them in the wedge of light from the Broken Promise's open doorway when he halted briefly to put on his top-coat against the chill dampness of the night air. The two dudes who, as he continued his unhurried walk, he heard cross the sidewalk and then begin to lead their horses in his wake.

When he reached the front of the stable he halted in the cone of light that after illuminating the sign dropped down on to the double doors and the area of street before them. He used the stock of the Colt Hartford to bang on the stable doors.

"Yeah, what you want?" a man called grumpily.

"My horse. Black stallion. Negro brought him to you early this afternoon."

"Your horse?" There was surprise in the voice now. As the two dudes reached the edge of the patch of light and stopped: the shorter one eyeing Steele quizzically while his partner looked down at his mud-spattered boots and pants cuffs and then scowled at Steele as if he blamed the Virginian for the heavy rain of the afternoon which had turned the street into a mire and spoiled his appearance.

"And saddle, and bedroll," Steele called. "The three fellers down at the Broken Promise made a mistake."

"Well, I never," the surprised liveryman growled.

"But they did, so you want to bring out my horse?" He nodded toward the dudes. "It seems I have some business to attend to out here."

"You're mighty cocksure of yourself, ain't you, mister?" the one concerned about his muddy boots and pants snapped.

"We haven't exactly hidden our interest in Mr. Steele, Niles," the shorter one put in.

"I don't mean that, Craig. I mean the way he got a whole saloon full of guys mad at him and then he comes and stands under a light like some target in a friggin' shootin' gallery."

"Self confidence, Niles. That's not the same as being cocky. And confident, too, that if there was trouble, he could rely on some help." He touched the brim of his derby hat. "My name is Craig Powell and this is Niles Coe. We represent Mr. John C. Cline."

One of the stable's double-doors was dragged open as Powell spoke, and an old and stoop-shouldered man with a bushy and drooping mustache started to lead out Steele's stallion. Then he stopped and did a fast double-take at all three men on the street.

"You fellers gotta be talkin' about the man they call Ace Cline, ain't you?" the elderly liveryman said with a quiver of excitement.

"You got big ears, old man!" Niles Coe said flatly.

Steele took over the reins of the stallion and stopped to check on the tightness of the cinch as the beginnings of a smile became frozen into an expression that was close to fear on the face of the old-timer.

"I'm a poker man, mister," the liveryman whined. "Don't play much now, but I follow games. Especially the big ones. Ace Cline, he only used to play in the biggest. Did I say somethin' wrong?"

"Easy, mister," Craig Powell said in a tone of voice that was obviously supposed to placate the old man, but sounded more menacing than that of the unsubtly harsh Coe. "I said something wrong. You just have to be sure you don't repeat it. In the event the wrong people hear you."

"And if they do, we'll get to hear about it," Coe took up the threat in a tone that he attempted to match with that of Powell. And failed. "After which we will come to visit with you. You want me to tell you more?"

"Gee, no."

"So get back in there with the rest of the horse-shit," Coe snarled.

41

The old man did so, back stepping fast and slamming the door after him. To shut off the brighter light, the spilled heat from a stove and the pleasant aromas of horses and hot coffee.

"Do you represent Cline in anything else except scaring the hell out of defenseless old men?" the Virginian asked, satisfied with the set of the saddle. He slid the Colt Hartford into the boot and swung smoothly astride the stallion.

"A guy with a bad mouth could get to swallow the teeth in it!" Coe said, looking and sounding the same as when he had sent the liveryman back into the stable.

"Shut up, Niles," the soft-spoken Powell muttered, although his frown of displeasure was directed toward the Virginian. "To make it *touché*, like the French say, Mr. Steele, can you play your mean poker in a real big game? With players who'd make those jokers down at the Broken Promise seem like a bunch of old biddies at a bridge club meet?"

"Poker's poker, feller," the Virginian answered. "Whether it's penny ante or the sky's the limit."

"He talks like a professional, Craig," Coe muttered as he mounted his gray gelding and, grimacing his distaste for the chore, used a silk handkerchief to try to wipe the mud from his pants and boots. "Way he plays, like I told you."

"Shut up, Niles." Again Powell did not look at his partner. "It's cold out here on the street,

Mr. Steele. And you look like you could use a shave and a hot bath maybe?"

"Something else, too."

"A drink? You're the kind of player who doesn't mix liquor with cards. I noticed that."

"I never mix liquor with anything. Hungry is what I am."

"No problem. If Mr. Cline likes you he'll have his chef cook you up a fine dinner. And if it doesn't work out, it's not far to ride back to the city from the house. Lots of hotels and lots of restaurants in Chicago. And the finest food in the country bar none if a man knows where to eat."

"Maybe he knows the city, Craig," Coe said.

"If he knew it, we'd know him," Powell said shortly and mounted his horse—the way he did this and the way he sat in the saddle showing that riding was not something he was good at or enjoyed. "What do you say, Mr. Steele?"

"What have I got to lose?" the Virginian asked with a shrug.

"Some time is all. Against which you stand to gain a great deal. Mr. Cline has been called many things, but never ungenerous."

They moved off, Niles Coe taking the lead and Steele and Powell riding side by side tight behind him. The kerosene lamp lighting the livery stable sign was suddenly darkened, by the old-timer reaching out from a hatch in the hayloft. Patches of yellow continued to show at the breath-misted windows of the Broken Promise Saloon. And were supplemented for a few moments when the doors were opened to let out a man. This after the trio of riders had turned a corner and the sounds of the horses hooves moving through mud had faded. The man stood for a moment on the sidewalk, gazing malevolently along the dark and empty street toward the corner where the horsemen had gone from sight and hearing. Then he sucked at the back of his left hand, spat out red-stained saliva and took long, angry strides toward the now un-lighted livery stable.

"We were downtown when we heard about the game at the Broken Promise," Craig Powell said suddenly after they had ridden in silence for perhaps five minutes—Steele and Coe keeping careful watch over their surroundings while the soft-spoken and always self-controlled dude rode in an attitude of thoughtful relaxation.

The sprawling city still had a solid cover of low rain cloud which allowed no pinprick of starlight or even a hazy impression of the shape of the moon to penetrate. But, although Niles Coe set a course that swung clear of the center of Chicago, the streets he took were never totally dark. Always there was a saloon, a store, an office where work went on late or a scattering of houses with light-spilling windows which kept pitch darkness at bay.

"Why?" Steele asked, aware of the expert way in which Coe was checking the shadowed places between the areas of light but, as always, not prepared to trust his life completely to somebody else.

"Why?" Powell asked, puzzled.

"Did you hear about a no-account poker game in a rundown place like that saloon?"

"Yes, of course. Well, because we let it be known that we were looking for a fine player of the game who has not yet made a reputation for himself in poker circles. And, Mr. Steele, when somebody is searching for just such a player as this, places like the Broken Promise are just the right places to look."

"Hey, Craig, you already said too much back at the stable," Coe complained. "I figure you oughta let Mr. Cline tell the rest. It he takes a shine to this guy."

"You're a worrier, Niles," Powell accused with a sigh. But he took account of what the taller man had said. For he abruptly changed the subject, to ask: "What has brought you to Chicago, Mr. Steele?"

"This horse I'm riding, feller."

They were passing a large lighted display window of a late-opening grocery store, so that the Virginian was well able to see Powell's facial response to the answer he had given. And to Niles Coe's short burst of harsh laughter. The man scowled dangerously, the expression deepening in intensity at the sound of his partner's laughter.

"Shut up, Niles," Powell rasped, and then leaned to the side to whisper to Steele so that the man in front could not overhear: "Put me down again, mister, and I'll show you how a real knife artist operates."

He sat up straight in the saddle again and brought his facial muscles under control: but

45

kept his lips compressed as if he didn't trust himself to talk and maintain his hastily regained composure.

He had a classically handsome face, the features in perfect proportion and finely chiselled. Probably in his youth he had been girlishly pretty, but during the early years of adulthood as he started to shave and to experience some of the harsher facets of life there had been a hardening up of the outlines of the face, a toughening up of the otherwise unblemished skin and a premature engraving of patterned furrows in the newly toughened skin at the sides of the eyes and the mouth. He had jet black hair, trimmed somehow too neatly at the back of the neck. When he scowled his lips were pulled taut enough to almost disappear. He had green eyes that seemed to look without seeing—as if the mind in back of them was engaged in a daydream of better times in a better place. But even after such a short acquaintance, Steele guessed that the eyes of the man told a constant lie: that Powell saw everything and overlooked little that was of importance to him.

He was about six feet tall, and slimly built. Not physically strong, maybe, but probably very fast to move. Cunning, like an animal which knows its limitations in the kingdom of the wild: but capitalizing to the full on the talents of which he was aware.

In appearance his partner provided a complete contrast. For he was at least six feet three inches tall, weighed in the region of two hundred and twenty pounds, was broad-shouldered and barrel-chested and had the kind of face that had probably been considered ugly by everyone except his parents when he was six months old.

Niles Coe had a square face with small and widely spaced brown eyes, a misshapen nose with a prominent bridge and a bulbous end, a thick-lipped mouth filled with crooked and uneven-sized teeth and a red-blotched complexion. He wore his black hair longer than Powell and sported broad sideburns.

He looked—and had acted so far—like a man of few talents. Of which horseback riding was one. And talking tough was another.

His suit was cut in precisely the same style as that of Powell, but was gray whereas that of his partner was dark blue. They wore identical black derby hats, plain white shirts and string ties.

At first glance an ill-matched pair, they probably complemented each other. Perhaps with qualities other than the obvious ones of brain and brawn.

Something they had in common with each other—and with Steele, too—was an ability to share silence in company without self-consciousness. And after it had been accepted that it would be better for all concerned if business discussions were delayed until later, they all three rode easy with their private thoughts.

Heading north through the east side of the city, sometimes along dirt streets made muddy by the rain and at others riding on paved avenues which caused the clop of hooves to resound eerily between the façades of the flanking buildings. Until eventually they emerged into open country with the vast flatness of Lake Michigan to the right of the trail and an expanse of low and timber-covered hills beyond meadowland on the left. The meadows were enclosed by neat, white-painted fencing which gleamed in the darkness. And some of them were bisected by gravel driveways which started at gates in the front fences and went from sight in the trees of the hillsides and folds between. Here and there among the timber there were sprinklings of distant yellow lights to mark the positions of secluded houses.

"Almost there now," Craig Powell announced gratefully, shifting his seat in the saddle as Coe swung off the public trail, reined in his horse, leaned down to release a fastening and used a muddied boot to push open a five-bar gate.

"Enter, and see how the other half lives," the sourly grinning Coe invited and overacted a gesture of ushering the other two riders through the opening and on to the driveway.

"I'd guess you've had a wide experience of seeing how both halves live, Mr. Steele," Powell said, his tone adding a light query to the comment. And he smiled knowingly, with a pretense at friendliness, as if he had never even considered warning the Virginian that he thought himself the more expert with a knife as a weapon.

"That a necessary qualification for the man your boss is looking for, feller?"

"I told you!" Powell hissed, angered by the

48

tone and content of Steele's response—and by the way Niles Coe grinned as he caught up to ride in line on the other side of the Virginian. "Don't put me down in front of—"

He carried his knife in a spring-loaded sheath on the left side of his chest. And he was certainly fast in going for it and sliding it smoothly out of the sheath and from under his suit jacket. But he had made the mistake of announcing his intention. By word, tone and facial expression. So that Steele was able to begin his counter just a part of a second after Powell started to make his move.

A crude move, but effective against a poor horseman, riding close enough to reach, whom he did not wish to come to any real harm. He simply withdrew his left foot from the stirrup, kicked his leg forward, then brought it back wide to crash his heel into the front of Powell's shin: then as the injured man yelled in pain and surprise, his right foot slipping from the stirrup, Steele leaned across and shoved the man hard with a gloved hand.

Craig Powell's cry became shriller and louder as he was unseated from the saddle and toppled hard to the ground on the far side of his horse. The knife sailed out of his grasp as he flailed the air with his arms in an effort to bring his tumble under some kind of control and break his fall. As his horse—a skittish brown thoroughbred stallion—bolted up the driveway, panicked by the outburst of sound and motion.

Then, as the crash of gravel spraying hoofbeats diminished, Niles Coe began to laugh:

gazing down with glinting eyes at his partner as Powell struggled painfully to his feet. But all signs of pain were gone from the man's handsome face as he came fully erect—wiped away by a glower of embittered rage which he shared equally between the noisily amused Coe and the impassive Steele. A fury so intense that it left him unable to speak for long moments. Until his partner interrupted the laughter to blurt:

"Man, did you get put down that time, buddy!"

Powell powered an animalistic snarl into his throat to break the grip of the constriction on his vocal chords. And now fixed his unblinking gaze on the unmoving face of the Virginian.

"Niles is too dumb to realize this is no laughing matter," he said slowly and distinctly. "But it seems like you know better, mister."

A purse of the lips before: "Never have been able to laugh at a clown, feller. Just doesn't appeal to my sense of humor."

Powell made an instinctive move to reach for his knife. But recalled in time that he had tried this and lost the weapon as a result.

"Hey, Craig," a suddenly subdued Niles Coe said, "you ride my horse up to the house while I look for your blade, uh?"

"Go to hell, dumbo!" his partner snarled. "You couldn't find your own fat nose unless you had a mirror to look in."

He started to search in the grass at the side of the trail, kicking angrily at the turf.

"I tell you somethin' for nothin', mister," Coe rasped softly as Powell's boot located the missing knife and he stooped to pick it up. Then carefully wiped the moisture off the blade before he thrust it back into the sheath. And started to stride up the driveway.

"You will?" Steele heeled his horse forward.

Coe did likewise. "You just made a bad enemy, mister."

"Is there any other kind?"

"I mean real bad, mister."

A nod, and a grim smile. "Got you. He isn't just bad. He's terrible."

Chapter Four

John C. Cline sat in a winged, high-backed chair to one side of a blazing log fire and looked across the big room with unconcealed distaste as the woman opened the tall double-doors to admit Powell, Steele and Coe.

"What the hell?" he exclaimed. "I know time's getting short, you guys, but if we're that desperate, let's forget the whole frigging thing!"

He looked like a most unsavory character to deal with. A grossly fat man with more chins than could be counted without intense concentration on the futile chore. About sixty-five, he had silver hair which was thinning and smooth, pink-toned skin which was stretched taut by excess flesh between his rounded features. His eyes were blue and bright and his mouth was shaped in such a way that it looked as if it would be able to alter from a scowl to a broad grin and back again so fast that people with him could miss the changes unless they were paying close attention. He weighed at least three hundred pounds or maybe even fifty pounds more than this: the enormous load hanging obscenely on a framework that stood no taller than five and a half feet. He was dressed in a vividly crimson pure silk robe and carpet slippers of the same color trimmed with expensive-looking fur. Which left his thick neck, a large vee of his bulging chest and the short, fat lengths of his calves and ankles bare. And the skin displayed here was as smooth, pink and hairless as that of his face.

The room in which he sat, its air over-heated by the burning logs, was luxuriously but impersonally furnished: with deep-pile carpets, over-padded leather armchairs and rosewood tables and cabinets. The panelled walls were sparsely hung with oil paintings and there were a few porcelain ornaments spread about. So that it looked to the Virginian like a room in a house that Cline was renting. Featured with a few frills supplied by a rich owner who knew where to draw the line between comforts for himself and for others who could afford but did not deserve the best.

The woman with long, blond and greasy looking hair who stood by the doorway wearing a petulant expression also had the appearance of being rented. She was in her mid-twenties with a slender, generously curved body

54

wrapped in a cheap and garishly multi-colored robe. The fingernails of the hand which she used to clutch together the plunging neckline of the robe were painted bright red. As were her thick, pouting lips. There was also artificial color on her eyelids and cheeks. If she was the best that Cline's money could buy, the enormously fat man apparently had little use for beauty.

"He's not what he looks to be, Mr. Cline," Powell said quickly as the bright blue eyes of the man by the fire became fixed in a stare upon the Virginian's impassive features.

"If I don't look hungry, your boy's right, feller," Steele added.

"What you don't look is the kind of man I need, mister!" Cline countered sternly. But then his fleshy face broke out into a grin and several gold teeth glinted in the fissure between his taut drawn lips. "However, young man, appearing to be what one is not and vice versa is an essential skill for the best poker players. And you claim to number yourself among these?"

"What about her, Mr. Cline?" Powell asked anxiously, stabbing a finger toward the woman.

"Go warm my bed, Laverne," Cline ordered.

"Can she cook, feller?" Steele asked.

"I have a chef to do that, young man."

Steele nodded and looked at the girl. "Be grateful if you'd stop off in the kitchen on the way and have something fixed for me."

"I ain't here to run no messages for every—" the woman started and her diction was as crude as that of Niles Coe.

"Do like he tells you, Laverne," Cline cut in on her. "Tell Frenchie to make it what I had awhile ago." He arched his eyebrows in Steele's direction. "Steak with potato salad and some apple pie and ice cream to follow all right, young man?"

"Sounds like heaven and I'm not dead yet," the Virginian said, sharing a quiet smile between Cline and the woman.

"Don't tempt providence, mister," Powell rasped close to Steele's ear as he moved to close the doors in the wake of the scowling woman.

"Laverne is just a whore," Cline said, waving for Steele to cross the room and sit in a matching winged chair on the other side of the hearth. "Even men of the highest tastes are allowed to roll in the gutter on occasions. Wouldn't you say so?"

Before he sat down, the Virginian took off his topcoat and draped it across his lap, then rested the Colt Hartford on the coat and an arm of the chair. Powell and Coe stayed over by the doorway, on either side of it.

"You asked me for one opinion already, Mr. Cline. No, I don't claim to be among the best poker players. Because I've never played with the men everyone says are the best."

Cline rested his elbows on the arms of his chair and pressed the tips of his splayed fingers and thumbs together in front of his many chins. "And who do they say are the best, young man? Is the name Ace Cline still spoken with awe?"

"Subject never came up in any conversation I've ever held."

The fat man's smile suddenly vanished and he frowned: "Nonsense. People who play poker for a living—even at your level—talk about very little else but poker. So how can you sit there and—"

"I don't play poker for a living, feller."

Cline snapped his head around to glare across the room at the two men flanking the doorway. "What the hell is this?" he demanded, his pinkish complexion shading to red. As he pushed out both hands in a silencing gesture toward Powell who had opened his mouth to speak. "You two come in here looking like you've been wading in the lake. You muddy up the carpets and you bring with you an unwashed and unshaven guy who smells like he hasn't been out of his clothes for a week. Who flaunts a frigging rifle. Who demands to be fed. Who . . . who . . . Damn, and he ain't even a pro player which is what I sent you guys out to frigging—"

Cline was one of those late and often self-taught men who were able to maintain a façade of being cultured and well-educated for as long as they could keep from getting angry. And he was angry now, allowing his accent to slip.

"But, Mr. Cline, he's better than a whole bunch of pros I've seen!" Powell cut in. "And it's better to have some one like him who no one who's anyone will know. Kind of a dark horse who'll keep the others guessing and—"

Now Cline cut in on Powell, but snapped his attention back to Steele. "Where'd you learn to play poker?"

"In my father's house."

"Who was your father?"

"Ben Steel of the Steele Plantation in Virginia."

"I never heard of him."

"He never made mention of you, feller."

Cline pursed his lips and looked on the point of taking offense at the barbed response. But then he simply shook his head and with an anxious frown muttered: "I don't like this. Not one little bit." He started to wring his hands together, very hard, as if they were ingrained with dirt and he was soaping them. He stared down at where his hands were moving in his lap, then up at the Virginian. And there was a look close to pleading in his bright blue eyes when he asked: "Tell me about yourself, son? The biggest game you ever played in? Where it was? Who else was in the game? How much was involved?"

Looking at the fat old man and listening to his suddenly whining voice, Steel wondered briefly whether John C. Cline was insane or merely frantic with anxiety. But then he decided it didn't matter: as he shook his head and rose from the chair.

"You'd better have your boys go out and find you somebody else—"

Craig Powell pulled out his knife silently. A bone in the finger of his throwing hand cracked in the act of releasing the knife. But Steele was unaware that he was standing on the narrow line between life and death until he heard a thud and wrenched around to see the knife buried to its hilt in the leather-covered padding of his arm chair.

By the time the Virginian had raked his gaze over to the door Niles Coe had drawn a Frontier Colt. Jerked it from the waistband of his suit pants at the small of his back: and he cocked the hammer as he achieved a rock steady aim at Steele.

"If we do have to get somebody else," Powell rasped with a vicious sneer twisting his lips, "it will be because our first choice met with an accident."

Knuckles rapped on one of the double doors. "The dinner you ordered, *monsieur*," a man with a thickly accented voice announced.

"I always think that hearty meals are wasted on condemned men," Powell added after the interruption from beyond the closed doors.

"Damn it, man, you stand to get ten per cent of the biggest pot ever seen in a game of five-card draw!" Cline urged, almost in full control of himself again. "And I'll be carrying the financial risk of backing you! Surely I have a right to know what kind of man it is who's betting with my money?"

"*Monsieur!*" the man beyond the doors called, a note of irritation in his voice. "The food, it is getting cool!"

"Come on in," Steele invited as he dropped back into the chair, withdrew the knife from the arm padding, looked briefly with mild interest at the slender metal blade, circular ivory hilt and contoured wood handle: and then tossed the weapon among the burning logs.

59

"Why, you crazy sonofa—" Powell started to rasp.

As both doors were pushed open with a thud by a short, bald-headed man trundling a two-tiered dumb waiter: with a covered tray on the top and a bottle of wine and a crystal glass beneath. For a few moments, the man who was dressed in white-and-blue-striped shirt and pants under an all-white apron looked almost as angry as Powell. But then he saw the aimed revolver in Niles Coe's big fist and he became nervously agitated.

"The meal you ordered, *monsieur*," he said hurriedly. "For you or for one of these gentlemen?"

"Me, feller," Steele replied.

"What you want me to do, Craig?" Coe asked.

And the chef swallowed hard as he started to move and pulled up short, realizing that to get the dumb waiter over to where Steele sat beside the hearth, he would have to cross the line of fire.

"You'll put that damn gun away, that's what you'll do, Coe!" Cline snarled. "And remember who pays you. Yes, Frenchie, the meal is for Mr. Steele here. Set it out on that table. And then have Laverne run a tub of hot water for our guest. He'll be staying in the blue room. Yes, the blue room is about the best we have to offer."

The enormously fat man had started out with a tone of high anger. But he finished up with a smile on his fleshy features and his voice was calm. If he saw Coe look with narrowed eyes at Powell and receive a nod before the Colt was returned to its holster under the suit jacket at the back, he elected to show no reaction to it. Instead, he touched his fingertips together again and directed his smile at the Virginian over the top of his hands. As Frenchie, not entirely placated nor free from anxiety, pushed the dumb waiter over to the specified table and began to unload it.

"Ten per cent of the biggest pot ever is what got to you, is that right, young man?" Cline asked and there was a glint of triumph in his eyes and a sound of it in his voice.

"Money's the reason I do most things, feller," Steele answered, and rose to cross to the chair which the Frenchman was holding for him at the laid table. He carried the Colt Hartford with him and, as at the Broken Promise Saloon—which seemed half a world away from the expensive and luxurious surroundings in which he now sat—he rested the rifle against the chair. "Grateful to you," he said to the chef, and eased the gloves off his hands. Then took off his hat and dropped his gloves inside before placing it on the floor.

"Weren't you told you would be well paid?" Cline asked, with a glower towards Powell.

"I told him he could expect you to be very generous, Mr. Cline." The good-looking, slimy built man with the vacant green eyes was still angry about the arrogant way in which the Virginian had reacted to the hurled knife. But he was struggling hard to control his emotions.

Motivated by something other than fear of the fat man.

Niles Coe seemed to have lost interest in what was happening and was examining his fingernails, as if checking that he had not broken any of them when he drew the gun.

"The girl will not like having to do the work of a maid, *monsieur*," Frenchie warned as he pushed his cart back across the room.

"But she'll damn well do what I've told you to tell her!" Cline snapped.

"No need," Steele put in, after he had chewed a piece of the tenderest steak he had ever tasted and swallowed it. "Reckon you'll pay expenses plus the percentage?"

"Yes, I suppose so," Cline said, surprised.

"Then I'll stay at a city hotel."

Cline was surprised by this, and looked as if he might get angry again as Powell, the chef and even Coe eyed him expectantly. Then he shrugged. "Just as you wish, Mr. Steele. Although you would be far more comfortable here, I assure you."

"The house looks fine, feller. It's just that I'm not too fond of some of the furnishings."

There were stretched seconds of heavy silence. Which ended when the Frenchman pushed out the dumb waiter and, as he closed the doors behind him, Niles Coe posed: "Hey, Craig, he talkin' about us?"

Cline sprang his fingertips apart, vented a short, sharp sigh and clapped his hands together. "Enough of this stupid bickering. It seems obvious to me that you, Mr. Steele, and my men have not got off on the right foot. I neither know nor care about the reason for this. But if we are to do business together—"

"Same reason you and I got off on the wrong foot, feller," the Virginian cut in. "Way I see this, you need me more than I need you. Matter of fact, until a few minutes ago when you mentioned a figure, I wasn't sure I needed you at all, Mr. Cline. Now that being the case, it seems to me that you should be giving me some answers instead of questions. To see if our needs can be evened out."

"You got a nerve, Steele!" Powell snarled. "Sitting here eating Mr. Cline's food and enjoying the hospitality of his—"

"Shut up, Craig," the fat man growled, and Coe had to turn away and cover his thick-lipped mouth with a hand to try to hide his enjoyment of another put-down for Powell—his pleasure probably heightened by Cline's use of one of his partner's favorite expressions. "Steele's right. I was under the impression that you had told him what was required of him."

"Told him enough, way I figured it," Powell muttered, fighting what had become a constant battle to suppress his urge to rage. "That you wanted him to play a big poker game for you and that he'd be well paid."

Cline nodded. "That sums it up very well. It is precisely what I require of a top class poker player, Steele."

"Why?"

The fat man licked his fleshy lips with the tip of a pink tongue. A partially burned log moved heavily in the bed of the fire and flames and sparks leapt up into the blackness of the chimney. "The way you keep a rifle by you in much the same manner as Craig carries a knife and Niles a revolver, I would think you are skilled with the weapon?"

"Reckon I could hit a barn door from ten paces with it," Steele allowed, between mouthfuls of crisp green salad that tasted like it had been picked from the garden only minutes ago.

"And you have a reputation for your skill as a rifleman?"

"Some people know about it, I daresay."

"The same with me and playing cards, young man," Cline went on, his tone morose and his fleshy face taking on the shape of a mournful frown. "Ace Cline is what I'm known as and if you've never heard of me it's because you've never played cards with professional players in any one street town or sprawling city east of the Mississippi. Trouble is, I can't cut the mustard any more. Not in the big time. Could sit down across from you right now and play the way I always used to. But if someone like Sam Sinclair, Lowell Banning, Willard Sloan or Justin Ford was in on the game . . ." He licked his lips again and off the top one got some salt sweat beads which had started to stand out on his smooth, pink flesh. "Well, Steele, if them fellers or even just one of them was playing in the game, why I'd just go to pieces. I suppose you've played in games where men have cracked. Usually happens when they've lost more than they can afford."

Steele nodded, in agreement and understanding, as he swallowed the final mouthful of food and rattled his fork down on the empty plate. "One of those fellers you mentioned caused you to lose your nerve, uh?"

A nod, with the same mournful expression still in place. "Ford. At a game in Boston Massachusetts ten months ago. Took me for one hundred and fifty thousand dollars with a ten to the ace running flush against my nine to the king. In a game with no wild cards." He drew in a deep breath and blew it out with his bottom lip jutted forward: to direct the draft of cool air up over his sweat beaded face. Then he managed to draw a mask of impassiveness over his depression as he said flatly: "Haven't been able to play poker worth a damn since that night in Boston, young man."

Steele finished pulling his gloves back on. He had taken to wearing gloves during the war: perhaps to keep warm or to prevent getting blood on his hands, he could not remember. Then, for another reason he could not pinpoint, he had come to regard them as some kind of lucky charms: wearing them, winter or summer, when he suspected trouble. For a long time now, during the violent peace, he took them off when he ate or when he slept.

"If I found out I couldn't hit that barn door, feller, I wouldn't bother to carry the rifle any more."

"Just one final game, Mr. Steele," Cline said tensely, the look of pleading re-entering his bright blue eyes. And the fact that he used the courtesy title again was not lost on the Virginian. "Ford's in Chicago doing some business and he's found out I'm here renting this house. Now there hasn't been a big game since that one in Boston. Mostly because he hasn't had the time to play while he's been loud-mouthing all over about what happened. But there's gonna be a game tomorrow night at the Regency on Michigan Avenue. Sam Sinclair and Banning are coming in for it and Ford's challenged me to take the fourth chair. What I want you to do is to take the seat on my behalf and with me putting up the money."

"And to get a chair in the game, a man has to have a half million dollars on the table in front of him, Steele," Craig Powell growled. "And so with that kind of money involved, it's natural Mr. Cline should want to know more about you than the color of your eyes."

"Doesn't he trust you, feller?"

"What's that got to do with it?"

"Shut up, Craig!" Cline said again and this time Niles Coe found nothing amusing about it. "What Mr. Steele means is that you saw him play poker someplace and I should either trust your judgment or not. Right?"

This last was addressed to the Virginian who was still seated at the table before the empty plates and the full bottle of wine.

"Reckon so. Seems I played well enough to bring your boys from downtown to the wrong side of the tracks. And they liked what they saw at the Broken Promise enough to bring me here. I've heard your proposition, which is what I came here for. And I'll take that chair with you staking me. What color my eyes are and everything else about me now or in the past seems to me to be nobody else's business but my own."

"For half a million dollars, Mr. Cline wants to know—"

"Craig!" the fat man snapped, and paused to see if the tension which had built up inside his obese frame would drain away. But there seemed little chance of this, unless he was able to find some kind of safety valve he could trigger open. Powell scowled and Cline looked intently at Steele. "The money is unimportant. You'll have the half million entry stake and if it's needed—you tell me it's needed—there'll be an additional five million available. But I have to win, young man. I have to break Justin Ford. That's more important to me than life itself. And so you must surely understand that I have to be absolutely certain that you are the right man for the job."

Steele got up from the chair by the table, lifted his Colt Hartford and canted it to his left shoulder. "Only one thing certain about a poker game, feller," he said. "And that is that the result is always uncertain. I'll play for you, but I won't offer any guarantee about winning. And there's nothing I can tell you or you can find out about me that'll give you a guarantee."

As he moved closer to the doors, Powell and Coe side-stepped to stand in front of them: the shorter man glowering his emnity toward the Virginian and his less emotional partner expressing simple aggression because it was ex-

67

pected of him. Steele halted to look back over his shoulder to where the fat, pink, anxiously frowning, heavily sweating John C. Cline sat.

"You said Ford's staying at the Regency on Michigan Avenue in the city?"

A nod.

"I'll be there, too, if you still think you need me."

"For a man I'm given to understand is a first-class poker player, you look . . . Well, dressed like that you won't get into the hotel. It seems to me, Mr. Steele, that you are asking me to take a lot on trust."

"I'm not asking you for anything, feller," Steele said and faced front again. "Except to get these two out of my way. So I can get to a hotel and rest up. Maybe buy some fresh clothes if there are any stores open this late."

"Craig, Niles, I've had enough of your physical methods for one night. Step aside. Very well, Steele. I'll talk over this matter with Mr. Powell and I may or may not contact you at the Regency Hotel."

There was no longer any strain in his voice. And he sounded at his most cultured. As if he had made his decision and this allowed him to regain his composure without further effort.

"But it would have been very pleasant for both of us if you had agreed to stay here at the house," he went on. "I notice you did not drink the wine. Perhaps it did not appeal to you? But I have some very fine old brandy. Or port if you prefer it. Now there's a wine. And some really excellent cigars."

"He don't drink, Mr. Cline," Niles Coe muttered, and made it sound like a taunt. "Nor smoke, I bet?"

"Right, feller," Steele confirmed as Powell wrenched open one of the doors which gave on to a hallway as plushly and impersonally furnished as the large, fire-warmed living room of the rented house.

"And you don't sleep with women, either?" the slimly built, handsome man sneered, his lips seeming again to disappear above and below his gleaming white teeth.

"Well, I try not to," the Virginian drawled with the boyish smile that served to cut several years from his true age. "Whenever I'm fortunate enough to get one into bed with me, I do my best to stay awake."

Chapter Five

The rain was falling again out of the low sky
when Steele left the big house, swung astride
his horse and began the ride back into the city.
But the weather was not so bad as it had been
during the afternoon and early evening, except
when a gusting wind sprang up off the lake
from time to time to take hold of the droplets
and hurl them violently westward. But between
these noisy, flesh-stinging flurries, he was always aware of at least one man trailing him.

But since the man—or men—had begun to follow him before he was off the property sur-
rounding the house John C. Cline was renting,
the Virginian did nothing more about it than to
remain poised for retaliation to an attack, in the
event that Powell or Coe—or both of them—had
instructions from the fat man to do more than

simply trail him. Or had taken it upon themselves to even up a personal score.

Which meant that Adam Steele rode this trail into Chicago the same way as the one earlier in the day. The same way he rode every trail from almost the opening days of the war when he had been made aware that people were trying to kill him. Hunched against the chill and wetness of the lakeside weather, with his hat brim pulled down and his coat collar turned up, he rode at a steady, energy conserving pace. With his eyes constantly moving in their sockets, his ears strained to pick up the first sound of potential danger from beyond the range of his sight and with both hands lightly holding the reins. In an attitude which suggested he had not a care in the world—which just might trick a nearby enemy into over-confidence. A state of mind in which a man was most likely to make a mistake.

Nobody closed in on the lone rider out in the country between the lake and the lush pastures with wooded slopes in back of them. But he did not relax his alertness when he was back on city streets: in fact, was more aware of his vulnerability to danger in these alien surroundings. Not merely a new environment in the way that an area of desert or mountains—or wooded hills and lakeside—he had not ridden before might be strange. For his feelings about cities, their paved streets, high buildings and large populations, went deeper than this. And not just because of the bad times he had experienced in the few cities he had seen: Washington at the end of the war, New Orleans where a rich woman made a fool of him and he almost died, and San Francisco where Renita had entered—and left—his life. He probably had worse times and closer brushes with violent death far beyond the limits of any large city.

No. It was a matter of where a man could feel at ease and at home. And for a drifting man like Adam Steele that had to be anywhere he could hang his hat and lay his weary body down to sleep. Which he was able to do with relative peace of mind in any strange spot out in open country. Because he could be sure that, if he was not alone, he was sharing the terrain with no more than a handful of others: and it was easy to spot a potentially dangerous man in a small group. Whereas in a crowded city . . . ?

Despite the lateness of the hour, downtown Chicago was filled with people making the most of what the city had to offer in the way of Saturday night entertainment. Which seemed to Steele to be about the same as San Francisco, New Orleans and Washington. The same, too, he had to concede, as any much smaller western town or city which sought to attract visitors or to provide money-making diversions for those who came anyway. Albeit a greater variety and on a larger scale and, in the case of Chicago, amid surroundings of new buildings constructed of stone and steel after the old wooden ones were burned down by the fire of 1871.

So it was that in the falling rain, the droplets sparkling as they fell through the glows of countless lights, he rode between and in front of bars and dance-halls, theaters and gambling casinos, restaurants and arcades, bordellos pretending to be something they were not and others which made no secret of the wares which were for sale beyond their garishly painted signs.

The sidewalks were thick with moving people and the streets and avenues were choked with vehicles and horsemen. The rain acted to dampen the noise but not the spirits of the sellers and potential buyers of anything and everything that was for sale: on and off the streets. Probably, too, the fresh and clean water dropping out of the starless sky served to neutralize some of the smells which were an inevitable constituent of the atmosphere wherever so many people were crowded together. Certainly, Steele could smell only the staleness of old sweat on his body as he rode the paved, wet, heavily populated streets; looking for a store and trying—unsuccessfully—to spot the man or men who he felt sure still trailed him.

He chose to shop for what he required at a large double-fronted tailoring emporium on the intersection of South Wells and Van Buren Streets. Where he was able to hitch his stallion directly outside the broad, brightly lit entrance and keep the horse in sight for the whole time he was inside: except when he was in the fitting cubicle trying on the clothing he intended to buy. During such times the salesman, who was ingratiatingly pleased by the size of the order he was to get but nail-bitingly nervous of the way his customer kept a rifle beside him during the transaction, stared fixedly at the hitched horse. Ready to yell piercingly loud above the clamor of Chicago should anyone so much as glance enviously at the fine animal.

The Virginian spent over two hundred and fifty dollars on a completely new set of clothing, from boots up to hat and from Long Johns out to a sheepskin topcoat. He was particularly pleased with this last, since it was a virtual replica of the coat which he had owned for many years between the end of the war and not so very long ago when it went up in flames aboard a burning sternwheeler on the Red River.

He had the excitedly smiling salesman wrap the purchases and tie them with twine so that he could hang the packages from the saddlehorn. Then he rode north on Wells to Madison Street, his sense of being watched as strong as ever, but unable to spot anybody—familiar to him or not—who paid him the slightest attention. On Madison between Clark and Dearborn Street there was a bath-house where for seventy-five cents, plus a quarter promised to a street urchin for taking care of his horse and saddlebags while he was inside, he was able to soap and scrub off many days of trail dirt, soak away some of the mild aches and pains of rough country riding and shave the bristles of a thirty-six-hour growth of beard.

Once again, the only cause people had to notice him was the fact that the Colt Hartford was never out of his reach. In this case, even when he was naked and submerged to his neck in hot, sudsy water.

When he emerged from the bath-house; clean, freshly shaven and attired in his newly purchased clothing—except for the silk scarf around his neck and the buckskin gloves on his hands—the young guardian of his stallion and gear had to do a double-take to recognize Steele as the same man who had promised the twenty-five cents for the horse-holding chore.

If the Virginian's shadower—or shadowers—were equally confused, he or they were as quick to recover as the dirty-faced, lice-ridden boy. At least, Niles Coe was on Michigan Avenue at the corner of East Eighth when Steele rode up to the impressive entrance of the six-story Regency Hotel. Coe was seated astride his gray gelding, pretending to be interested in something that was happening up the avenue at the intersection with Balbo as the Virginian swung down from his stallion under the shelter of the broad canopy that jutted out from the hotel façade at second floor level.

"You need stabling for your horse, sir?" a liveried doorman asked, then had to grab at the visor of his cap to keep it on his head as the wind gusted in off the lake again.

"Feed, water, curry and stable for two nights," Steele instructed, drawing the rifle from the boot and thrusting the reins into the hands of a younger, less ostentatiously uniformed flunky who was beckoned forward by the doorman.

Rain billowed across the broad avenue like an opaque curtain and then, as the wind dropped and visibility lengthened, Niles Coe could no longer be seen.

"I can have the rifle delivered to your room along with anything else you need from your gear, sir," the man who had charge of the stallion offered before Steele could turn away towards the doors which were held open by the one with more gold braid on his uniform.

"This goes where I go and when I go," the Virginian replied, canting the Colt Hartford to his shoulder. "Have the saddlebags sent. Name's Steele."

"Guests are not encouraged to display weapons in the public rooms of the hotel, sir," the doorman said. "It's a rule of the house."

"A rule's not proved until there's an exception to it," the Virginian countered and stepped across the threshold.

Off the chill, damp, semi-darkened street into the warm, dry, dimly-lit lobby of the Regency. As he crossed the thickly carpeted floor on which was set a mixed bag of arm and straight-backed chairs, a few tables and several free standing ashtrays, Steele's mind was invaded by a vivid recollection of the fat, informally dressed, frightened and frustrated John C. Cline sitting by the blazing log fire amid the luxury of his rented house. For although the lobby was more obviously designed and furnished to offer comfort to transients, it had something of the same atmosphere as the one where Cline sat and fretted.

The walls were wood-panelled in much the same style, the fabrics covering the soft furniture was a similar pattern and even the lamps hanging from the ceiling fixtures were only slightly different in design. The sole striking dissimilarity seemed to be that instead of an open log fire, the Regency lobby was heated by two enclosed stoves.

But the two rooms nonetheless shared a common atmosphere, created by a distinct impression of good quality allied with the hard wearing characteristics of both furniture and decorations.

The room in the rented house had been more crowded when Steele was there than the lobby of the hotel. Here there was just a woman who may or may not have been a whore sitting in one of the most comfortable looking armchairs and a tall, stoop-shouldered, thin-faced man with weary eyes standing behind the long desk at the back of the lobby.

"Sir, you should not carry a—" the desk clerk opened anxiously, his tone matching the expression that crowded the fatigue from his eyes as soon as he looked away from the woman and saw that the newcomer had a rifle sloped to his shoulder.

"I heard," Steele interrupted. "So the sooner you give me a room number and a key the quicker the gun will be out of sight."

The woman had been dozing and the voices jerked her awake. She was disorientated for just a moment, then quickly worked an alluring smile on her hard, almost attractive face as she patted her dyed red hair and then smoothed the skirt of her dress so that the fabric contoured her thighs. She had a few more years of living behind her than Laverne, but on a scale of ten she out-classed Cline's bought woman by at least five in looks and deportment.

Or perhaps, Steele found himself thinking as he signed the register the desk clerk turned for him, it was just that Laverne purposely set out to hook a different kind of trade.

"If you want to make that a double room, stranger, I'm free," the red-headed whore in the tight-fitting black dress invited.

"You don't really mean that, do you, lady?" Steele asked, taking the key to room 101 which the clerk had brought up from under the desk top.

"But you know what I do mean, don't you? I'm open to any reasonable offer." She stood up from the armchair and now her hands tugged at the skirt of her dress, to make sure the bodice hugged tightly to her jutting breasts.

"Is Miss La Salle bothering you, sir?" the desk clerk asked. "We allow certain young ladies of her type to frequent the lobby as an additional service to the guests, sir. But if they are bothersome, the staff have instructions to remove them from the premises."

He spoke in the tone of a man saying something of which he did not approve. But when Steele shifted his gaze from the ready-to-be-worried, sensually preening whore to look back at the clerk, he saw that the man with the cadaverous face above the sagging shoulders was not disapproving of the woman's presence. For there was a glint of longing tinged with regret in the sunken eyes as they gazed for a final part of a second at Miss La Salle. The same expression, perhaps, which the Virginian had mistaken for weariness when he had first seen the man watching the woman.

"Reckon she's bothering you a whole lot more than she bothers me, feller," Steele replied as the desk clerk controlled the outward response to his emotions.

"Ruddy was wounded way back in the war, stranger," the whore explained in a sympathetic tone. "He still gets to feeling the need but there isn't any way he can be helped."

"Nancy, you don't have to tell everyone who comes to the hotel!" the clerk snapped, his composure falling away again. But he managed to regain it fast, his Adam's apple bobbing. "I'm sorry . . ." He turned the register around to read the name written by the name guest: "Mr. Steele, sir. If there's nothing else I can do for you, I'll ring for a boy to show you up to your quarters."

"Nothing, feller. And I can find my way to the room."

"What about me, sir?" the whore asked as the Virginian turned to head for the foot of stairs at one side of the lobby. "Is there anything I can do for you?" Then she worked a sympathetic tone back into her voice—but now it sounded forced. "And you'll be helping Ruddy as well as having a really good time."

"Don't drag me in again, Nancy!" the desk clerk growled.

"Aw, come on, Ruddy," she countered. "It must be easier for you when there isn't a woman around you."

"I'm not saying it isn't, but—"

"See, sir!" Nancy La Salle called up the stairway.

Steele halted, turned his head slowly and looked down at the man and woman in the lobby with mild scorn. "How much of the take do you get for your part in this double act, feller?" he asked.

"I beg your pardon—"

"Aw, the hell with it!" the whore interrupted gruffly, and dropped ungracefully back into the armchair. "I said at the start this was gonna be one of them slow Saturday nights, didn't I?"

Ruddy abandoned the look of injured dignity and expressed genuine anxiety. "You won't report this matter to the management, sir?"

"How much?" Steele insisted flatly.

Ruddy licked his lips. "Five cents on the dollar. But I don't make a great deal out of the—"

"But that's just because I only use him as a last resort on slow nights, mister!" Nancy cut in quickly, anxious that Steele should not draw the wrong inference from Ruddy's excuse for being a pimp—that she was not able to grab her fair share of the trade when it was available.

"Grateful to you," the Virginian directed towards Ruddy. "Just that I'm new to Chicago and didn't know the going rate in this town for enjoying another man's fantasy."

He faced front again and continued to climb the stairway.

"What the hell is that supposed to mean?" the clerk asked the whore.

"Don't ask me," Nancy La Salle answered in bored tones with a shrug as she settled down into the chair to try to get back to sleep. "You be sure to wake me in time for the rush hour, you hear?"

Steele's room was twenty yards down the corridor to the left at the top of the stairs and was as elegantly, comfortably and functionally furnished as the lobby. There was carpet on the floor, clean linen on the narrow but softly sprung bed, no dust in the clothes closet and fresh water in the pitcher in the bowl which stood on the bureau. To one side of the bed was a hard-seated, straight-backed chair. On the other side a table with a drawer in the front and a kerosene lamp on the top.

After Steele had lit the lamp, surveyed the room in its light, drawn the drape curtains across the rain bubbled window which looked down into an alley and taken off his topcoat, knuckles rapped on the door panel.

"Your saddlebags, sir," a youthful voice called.

"Door's unlocked," the Virginian replied as he sat down on the bed and started to ease off his left boot. Then: "Leave them over in the corner," he said to the lanky, blond-haired, pale-skinned boy of eighteen or nineteen who had taken charge of the stallion out front of the Regency.

"That be all, sir?" the boy asked pointedly after doing as instructed.

"All part of your job, isn't it?"

"Well, yeah, but—"

"Only tip for special service above and beyond the call of duty, son."

"Sir," the boy said, fast and nervous. "Ruddy, who's the night man on the desk takes care of that kinda thing. I think there's a woman down—"

"Not that kind of service. Some information."

A grin now. "If I can, sir."

"Mr. Justin Ford? You know him?"

"Of him, sir. He's a guest of the hotel."

"Describe him?"

The boy showed a worried frown again, which changed to one of deep thought as the moments slipped by. Then: "Tall as me, I'd say. That's six feet. But a lot older. Sixty or seventy, I'm not good at guessin' the ages of really old men. Real skinny. Like Ruddy but worse, if you know what I mean, sir? Oh yeah, and he's got some gray hair. Not much. Just at the back and a little curve over each ear."

"You know his room number?"

"We're not supposed to give out that kind of information to people unless—"

"Live a little dangerously, son," the Virginian urged. "No one will know and you'll be five dollars richer."

"Not a room, sir. A suite. Suite number one which is the best we have. Up on the sixth floor."

"Grateful to you," Steele said and held out the five-dollar bill towards the boy in the smart

83

livery. After it had been accepted with a smile and a nod, he added: "How about a Mr. Sinclair and a Mr. Banning? Are they guests of the hotel?"

The youngster's smile broadened to a grin of relief. "Oh, you have to be interested in the big poker game there's gonna be in the Illinois Room tomorrow. No, sir, those two gentlemen ain't staying at the Regency. I don't know where they are right now. May not even be in town. But I hear the fourth player—Mr. Ace Cline—he's got a rented house out on the lake shore north of Chicago. It sure should be some big—"

"Grateful to you."

He was stopped in mid-flow and was a little resentful that the Virginian did not share his degree of excited interest in the forthcoming card game. But the five spot which he pushed into a breast pocket of his uniform tunic salved his hurt feelings.

"No, sir. I'm grateful to you," he countered, and backed from the room, closing the door behind him.

Steele hurriedly pulled his boot back on, shrugged off his sheepskin coat, picked up the Colt Hartford and went to the door. He could not hear the boy's footfalls on the carpet in the corridor, so carefully eased open the door and looked outside: and was in time to see him turn a corner and go from sight at the far end from the head of the stairway.

The Virginian went in his wake, taking long strides—as silent as the boy on the carpet—and saw that what he had thought was a corner was in fact a recessed doorway with a notice on the panel proclaiming: STAFF ONLY. When he pushed open the door, he could hear the sounds of the boy's progress—footfalls descending a bare cement stairway. Dimly lit by a kerosene lamp with its wick set low which was positioned at the foot of the steps, around a right-angle turn. Just for a moment, the lamplight threw a dancing shadow of the boy against the gray stone wall. Then the shadow was gone, as a door opened, a draft of cold, damp air rushed in and reached high enough up the stairs to touch Steele's flesh. The door closed and silence filled the cold, poorly lit stairway area.

The Virginian allowed no more than two seconds to pulse into history before he started down the steps: unconcerned by the sound of his footfalls on the cement treads as he worked to get his bearings—thinking back over the change of directions he had made since he left his room. So that when he reached the foot of the stairs he knew that the door to the left would open on to some other part of the Regency's first-floor staff-only area: and the one on the right offered a way out to the broad alley which was overlooked by his room window.

He reached up to the lamp standing on a shelf to turn the wick and put out the light before he cracked open the door. The wind was gusting again and making low moaning sounds as it curved around sharp turns and forced itself between narrow crevices. But it no longer spat raindrops at the city, the dampness it spread before it merely a relic of its creation far out over the sea-like expanse of Lake Michigan. It was blowing in longer bursts and was stronger than before: reaching higher, too, attacking the cloud cover and winning. So that from time to time the moon showed briefly through the broken blackness and was reflected in the pools of water left in the potted surface of the alley by the earlier rains.

Another source of light was also reflected in a few of the muddy pools—yellow lamplight in perhaps a dozen different shapes which gleamed at the cracks around the doors of the livery stable and from splits and knotholes in the timbered façade of the building.

Steele stepped out of the hotel, closed the door behind him and moved diagonally across the fifteen-feet-wide alley to halt at one side of the stable's double-doors. For just a moment he indulged in regret at having left his topcoat upstairs. But then, as he put an eye to a crack just below a door hinge, he forgot the discomfort of the chill, biting wind which moaned down the alley and seemed to penetrate his new clothing as if the fabric were paper thin.

For he had achieved his vantage point in time to see the lanky, blond-haired boy grin broadly as he accepted and pocketed another bill. From a man who showed a different kind of grin: of evil intent rather than satisfied greed. A man of about sixty with red hair. Dressed in hard-wearing and hard-worn denim clothing. His right hand clean and flabby with excess flesh but marked by the scars of much heavy work in the past. His left hand almost completely wrapped in a rain-dampened dressing stained by the blood which had seeped through from the knife wound.

"Thanks, kid," Red Wilmot rasped. "Now beat it out to the front. And remember, ain't no one came around askin' questions about any of the hotel guests."

As the boy nodded and turned half around to come towards the door, Steele allowed himself a quiet smile of satisfaction: that he had been right to follow the mercenary youngster who, if he was prepared to break the rules for five dollars from one man would be ready to break them again for another inducement from another man. The Virginian did not indulge in surprise for long—surprise that the man who gave the boy more easy money was not Niles Coe.

He was about to pull back from the edge of the door, intending to seek cover in the narrow gap between one side wall of the livery and some kind of outhouse beyond, when he saw Wilmot draw the small gun from his pants pocket. A tiny double-barrel derringer that spat one of its bullets with a sound which reached the ears of the watching Virginian but carried no more than a few feet further into the alley before it was masked by the eerie moaning of the wind.

The bullet from the upper of the over-and under-barrels of the handgun had to travel just four feet to find the flesh of the grinning youngster. For Wilmot thrust the derringer out at full arm's length, sighting along the barrels' top like a target shooter. At such a short range, with a gun which had very little recoil, the no-longer grinning Red Wilmot was able to place the bullet accurately into the back of the boy's neck. On a slightly rising trajectory. The kind of shot which from a more powerful weapon would have driven the lead tearing from out of the back of the throat to perhaps explode a row of teeth before it came through the top lip.

But the boy died with his face unmarked by the manner of his passing. Except that, as the bullet penetrated his flesh, the look of pleasure was wiped from his features and he began another frown. An expression which was never completely born and set because he was dead on his feet less than a second after the bullet hit him. He started to fall rigidly, like a cut down tree. But then his muscles ceased to function and he collapsed limply into an untidy heap on the straw-covered dirt floor of the stable.

"You got a big mouth that works too cheap, kid," Wilmot muttered with a scowl as he pushed the release catch on the small gun and used his bandaged hand—the fingers of which were not encased by the dressing—to tilt up the hinged barrels section and extract the spent cartridge case.

It was while he was holding the open gun awkwardly in his injured hand and delving into his pocket for a fresh bullet with his good one that Steele wrenched open one of the stable doors and stepped into the building.

"What in—?" the redheaded man began, as the wind which spilled in from the suddenly opened door caused the kerosene lamp to swing from its hook in a ceiling beam—by turns bathing in light or plunging into shadow the man who had crossed the threshold.

But the man had a rifle, gripped one-handed and leveled from the hip. As he reached behind him with the other hand to bang the door shut. So that the surprised heavy loser from the Broken Promise Saloon guessed who had witnessed his killing of the boy: an eternity of time, it seemed, before he recognized in the intermittent lamplight the lower half of the face beneath the shadow of the hat brim.

"Steele!" he rasped, wrenched his good hand from the pocket, plucked the opened derringer from the almost useless hand and tried to snap and lock the barrels into the firing position.

Backing away from the body of the boy and the advancing Virginian. Sweating and trembling with anger or fear or both. No, not sweating. Steele saw that it was rainwater from his sopping wet hair that dripped from his forehead to his cheeks and then coursed down to his jawline.

"Talk is all, feller," Steele drawled as Wilmot was forced to come to a halt, his back hard against the front of an empty stall. "The boy is nothing to me—"

But the man from the Broken Promise was more frightened than angry: his mind locked on to one idea which the more powerful emotion would not allow to be dislodged. That Steele had seen him murder the boy—so Steele must also die. And there were other reasons for killing the man, too. But this one was strong enough for now.

At the second attempt he fumbled the catch home to fix the barrels of the over-and-under into place. He needed only one try to thumb back the hammer.

Which was when Steel shot him, pursing his lips to vent a soft sigh and looking at the man with eyes that revealed nothing of his feelings as he squeezed the trigger of the Colt Hartford. To blast a bullet across half the width of the stable between door and back stalls. The rifle held in a double handed grip now, but still at hip level. Aimed with effortless skill to put the bullet into the front of Wilmot's right arm and out of the back, just above the elbow joint.

Trapped inside the unheated, lamplit livery, the report of the rifle shot was shockingly loud. And caused most of the nine horses standing in the stalls to snort and snicker as they either reared or lashed out with their legs to thud the woodwork. Then the animals remained for long moments on the edge of panic, as the acrid taint of exploded powder penetrated the familiar scents of the stable.

"Christ, Steele, you're killing me a piece at a time," Wilmot groaned, leaning harder against the front of the empty stall as his pain-filled eyes shifted their gaze from the blood-stained hole in his jacket sleeve to his small derringer down on the floor between his boots and finally became fixed on the half-shadowed, half-clear-to-see face of the Virginian.

"You want to go all at once, feller?" Steele responded, and cocked back the hammer with a gloved thumb.

"No!" Wilmot choked out, and tried to thrust both hands forward as if in hope of deflecting the expected bullet. But only his left arm would move. His right one hung loosely at his side, exploding with pain when he called upon its muscles to work. He grimaced and stifled the urge to scream. He looked very old and very tough. More so than when he had been surrounded by friends ready to back his play at the saloon on the south side of the city. "Look, you gotta understand my point of view, Steele," he rasped through teeth clenched against the need to give vocal outlet to the pain that had turned his complexion gray. "I'm in deep to some pretty mean people for a lot of money. And I got Arnie and John into the same kinda hole. I don't come up with enough to pay off everyone, this ain't nothin' to what'll happen to me."

He raised his bandaged hand and glanced down at the blood-soaked sleeve of his coat.

"I've never believed what they say about people being able to die from a broken heart, feller," the Virginian drawled.

"Listen," Wilmot went on hurriedly, desperation in his tone and expression. "I just need eighteen hundred of that money you won. To give back to the guys I borrowed it off. You do that for me, and I'll pay you back. Any interest you care to name. It'll take a little time to raise, but I'll do it. Me and Arnie and John, we got friends all over this city. Like I told you down at the Broken Promise. You remember? I said if you needed any help in this city, we'd probably—"

"Tell me what you know about a man named Justin Ford."

Both doors of the stable were wrenched open and the previously subdued sounds of the now constantly raging wind were abruptly very loud. As the chill and damp of the weather rushed inside: tugging at the clothing of Steele and Wilmot, setting the lamp to swinging again and creating fresh urges to panic among the horses.

The Virginian turned instinctively towards the source of the disturbance. But with a section of his mind free to work out with calm logic that he had nothing to fear from the disabled Wilmot. So that when he looked at Craig Powell and Niles Coe standing in unmistakable attitudes of aggression on the threshold of the stable, he no longer felt the need to be concerned by the actions of the man with a knife wound in one hand and a bullet hole in the other arm.

But then there was no time for further reasoned thought. For he had to make a decision in part of a second. About whether to blast a bullet into the classically handsome Powell or to fire it into the broader, taller target of Coe. Or to take a third course of action and not shoot either man.

Both of them snapped their mouths wide to shout something. But the wind snatched the words off their lips and hurled them into the clamor of its own moaning and the sounds of the equine fear.

Then Coe went to the left, the Colt in his big fist spurting a stab of smoke in the wake of a bullet: as Powell moved in the opposite direction and swung his right hand forward from the shoulder to power a spinning knife through the air.

Wilmot groaned, but the Virginian had already realized the decision he made was the right one. It had been made on pure impulse but as soon as he eased his finger away from the rifle trigger he knew that Wilmot was the target. For there could be no other reason why the two men needed to shift their splayed-legged, ramrod stiff postures: to lean to either side and unbalance themselves. It could only be to aim the bullet and knife each side of him to find the flesh of the redheaded man.

He looked back at Wilmot in time to see the man become a corpse: his eyes closing and his mouth sagging open as his legs folded under him and he slid down the front of the stall. The bullet had drilled into his heart and the knife—with identical hilt and handle to the one Steele had tossed on the log fire—had buried its blade into Wilmot's right breast.

"He was reaching down for that crazy little gun, Steele," Craig Powell shouted as his partner struggled to pull the doors closed.

"Yeah, soon as you looked away from him,"

the taller and tougher looking man added as he completed his chore and closed out most of the sounds of the stormy weather. He showed his crooked teeth in a broad grin as he thrust the Colt back into its secret hiding place at the small of his back. "You got cause to thank the fine old firm of Powell and Coe, mister."

"I reckon," the Virginian muttered as he reached up with the rifle to halt the swing of the kerosene lamp, "that Powell and Coe could get to be an unlimited liability."

Chapter Six

"You don't believe what we said about that guy going for that gun, do you?" Craig Powell asked after the corpse of Red Wilmot and the young hotel employee had been taken out of the stable.

Niles Coe had drawn this chore and showed that in more ways than with a gun he could be a capable man to have around in time of trouble. There was a hay wagon parked out at the side of the livery and after hitching two horses in the traces he loaded it with the bodies and some bales of hay from the loft. Then he drove off along the alley and made a turn in the direction of Wabash rather than Michigan.

"Best we get rid of the kid, too," Powell had contributed as he retrieved his knife from the flesh of Wilmot, and Coe began his prepara-

95

tions. "No point in attracting any kind of attention from the law. The hotel people will just think he up and quit his job."

"No problem, old buddy. Plenty of room for a lot more than that in the lake," Coe replied gleefully.

Then, after he had dragged the bodies over to the doorway, his equally confident but less demonstrative partner started to erase the other physical evidence of violence—covering the blood-stained straw on the floor with fresh, rubbing dirt on the smear which marked the front of the stall and finally digging the Colt Hartford's wounding bullet from the woodwork. But not before Steele had picked up Wilmot's gun: and recognized it as a twin to the .41 Remington double derringer he had once owned. The gun, in fact, which he had used to fire the first shot in the violent peace.

He was still holding the little over-and-under, and reviewing the thousand and one memories which it triggered through his mind, when Powell turned from closing the door after watching Coe drive the rig along the alley, the moan and whine of the wind acting to cover the sound of the clopping hooves and turning wheels: when the question was posed.

"You care, feller?" Steele asked, and pushed the gun into a side pocket of his suit jacket, spoiling the line of the coat until he unfastened the buttons.

A shrug of the slender shoulders. "I guess it doesn't matter much. Way it's worked out, best to have that guy dead than still running around madder at you than ever."

"I reckon Cline wants me to play in the big game?"

"That's right."

"He made up his mind fast."

"Before you were out of the house." He was abruptly disconcerted. And had to control an impulse to anger. "You knew Niles and I were trailing you?"

"Knew somebody was. Wilmot had to be. From the Broken Promise to Cline's house and then to here. But somebody else to here who he knew about. Or he would have tried to jump me out in the country. Instead of going to all the trouble of finding out my room number from the kid and—"

"Shit, that's right!" Craig snarled, and directed his anger at himself. "How could he have known you were staying at the Regency unless he trailed us all the way?"

"But you got him in the end, feller," the Virginian muttered and started across the stable.

"We been told to look out for you!" Powell said quickly, holding his position in front of the closed doors, much as he had done in the big, fire-warmed room out at the house on the lake shore. "And that's just what we did! Like you said, that guy could've taken a shot at you easy outside of town! But he didn't, because we were around! Just like we were around when he thought he saw a chance in here!"

"Am I supposed to pay you the same way

Cline does?" Steele asked evenly as he came to a halt in front of the taller, slighter built man.

"Uh?" Disconcerted and puzzled both this time.

"You sound like a man making a sales pitch about how good you are."

The familiar expression of tightly controlled anger showed on his face again but without touching those dead looking green eyes of his. "Listen!" he rasped, then swallowed hard and squeezed his eyes tight shut for long moments. "All right. I guess that's what I am doing." There was a kind of distant shrillness in his voice. Until he opened his eyes and his tone began to match the look of anxiety which had spread across his handsome features. "Niles and me, we've been acting like a couple of prize chumps. It seems that we haven't been able to do a damn thing right since we laid eyes on you. Which isn't like us, Steele. We're the best there is. If we weren't, a man like Mr. Cline—who can afford the best, as you must realize—wouldn't keep us around.

"But you saw us in action awhile back. Saw the way we took care of Wilmot. Right or wrong about him going for his gun, we finished him with no slip-up. And now Niles is taking care of the mess these things always leave behind. That's more like us—more our style—than anything else you've seen us do. So I'd like you to keep that in mind. One or both of us is going to be somewhere close from now until when the game gets underway. So if anything like this happens again, you'll know whose side we're on when we show up. All I wanted to say."

He turned, pushed open one of the doors and strode quickly out into the wind-filled alley. Controlling his expression at least until he had whirled to hide it from the Virginian. But revealing by the ramrod stiffness of his back and the almost machine-like way in which he moved just how much effort this required.

"Trouble is, you showed up just in time to keep me from finding out whose side that is," Steele murmured as he stepped out of the stable and cracked his eyes against the force of the wind to gaze after the tall, long striding form of Powell.

He watched the man out of sight—until Powell turned a corner of the alley which would take him out on to Michigan Avenue. Then he closed the door of the stable and retraced his footsteps back into the hotel, up the service stairway to the second floor and then along the corridor. But he went beyond the door of his room and did not halt until he was at the head of the stairs, looking down on to the lobby. Where Ruddy was still at the desk, but reading a newspaper now. And Nancy La Salle had given up trying to go to sleep and was gazing with little hope towards the firmly closed entrance doors of the Regency.

"You still free, lady," he called down.

The desk clerk—who wore eyeglasses to read—looked briefly up the stairs at Steele with a rather disdainful expression in the set of his mouthline. As the whore got quickly to her feet, did the smoothing chore with her hands over her hips and smiled eagerly.

"Not free, but very reasonable," she replied, moving to the foot of the stairs and starting up.

Ruddy, who apparently got no share of this kind of deal, vented a low snort and returned to his study of the newspaper. While Steele started back along the corridor and was in his room and sitting on the only chair by the time Nancy reached the threshold.

She eyed the undisturbed bed with a puzzled expression. "What have you been doing, mister?" she asked as she came into the room, closed the door and leaned her back against it, in an attitude which caused her breasts and lower belly to push forward in an unsubtle display of the sexuality she had for sale. "Pacing up and down to try to lose the feeling that there's something else you need to do that way? You know what I mean, I suppose?"

She laughed suddenly, at the joke which was as crude as her stance. And the sound of her laughter was ugly: as ugly to hear as was her face to look at when her vividly painted lips gaped wide and the over-colored flesh crinkled around her eyes.

"What are your rates, lady?" Steele asked and the reference to money brought a moment of silence to the room.

During which the whore smiled a greedy smile, then rearranged her features into the expression which she knew from long experience made her look her most alluring. Particularly when the light came from below, as it did now with the lamp standing on the table. And at an anyway flatteringly dim level.

"I got different prices for different services, mister. And a special rate for an all-night trick. For all night you get everything you might—"

"How much did you make in the best ten minutes you ever had?"

"Don't you mean the best ten minutes one of my customers ever had, mister?" The ugly laugh again. Which not only did her face a disservice, Steele noticed. For the merriment also caused her body to quake, emphasizing the soft padding of excess flesh which for the rest of the time was camouflaged by the clever design of her dress.

"How much?" Steele insisted.

Her eyes beneath the green colored lids shifted from his uncommunicative face to his left hand. And seemed to gleam with evil avariciousness as the hand went into a pocket. In the stretched seconds of silence it was almost as if he could hear the workings of the whore's brain: reaching for figures and struggling to decide how high to pitch the price without spoiling her chance.

"Twenty dollars," she said at length, very quickly. And he saw her flinch, in expectation of a barrage of harsh words.

He withdrew the hand from the pocket, fisted around some bills. And looked away from the whore for a long time to separate thirty dollars. Which he tossed on the bed.

"Time and a half, lady. If you can supply what I need."

A smile. Of relief and pleasure. And just for a moment Nancy La Salle looked young and pretty. Perhaps even desirable. Until she raised her hands with the painted nails to her throat and began to unfasten the buttons of the high-necked dress.

"There isn't any way to please a man I don't know about, mister."

"Talk."

"While we're doing it? Sure. I can recite from the Bible, know enough bad words to keep it up for two minutes without repeat—"

"About other men."

An eager nod as the unbuttoning reached the start of the valley between her ample breasts. "No problem, mister. I've had more men do more things to me that you've had—"

"Justin Ford and John C. Cline."

Her hands suddenly stopped working and the expression of excited eagerness froze on her face. For long moments she stood like that, un-moving. The fixed expression making her look sick and the gaping neckline of the dress sug-gesting that part of the sickness was a fever which she hoped to relieve by loosening her clothing. Then:

"I'm in the prostitution business, mister. You wanna get laid real good, I'm your girl. You wanna die in company why don't you go to some graveyard and blow your own head off?"

She began to work with her hands again. But

this time her fingers were less fluid in their movements. As she pushed the buttons back through their holes. Anger, fear, resentment and disappointment crowded across her face, fighting for control of the features.

"Not for all the money in Chicago, uh?" Steele asked evenly.

"You got the idea, mister. Maybe I ain't got the best life there is, but it's the only one I got. And when I lose it, I want it to be the way I lived a lot of it. On my back in bed."

The Virginian nodded, pursed his lips and reached for the scattering of crumpled bills on the bed's counterpane. "The way you tell me nothing tells me something, lady," he said. "But it would be nice to know—"

Something hard and heavy crashed into the door. With enough force to smash the tongue of the lock from the bracket and swing the door wide open. Which sent Nancy La Salle staggering across the room with a choked cry of pain and shock bursting from her wide mouth. And her legs pumping and her arms flailing in an attempt to remain balanced through the enforced forward momentum. Until she was stopped suddenly by the iron-framed bed: when the sound from her throat became shriller and filled with pain from the impact of her knees crashing into the immovable obstacle. And she pitched face down across the narrow bed, covering the bills which Steele had abandoned collecting: to reach for the Colt Hartford as the door burst open.

"Kill you as easy as swat a fly!" a man shouted.

"Shut you frigging mouth, Nance!" another ordered.

The Virginian froze, half-turned towards the doorway and half towards where his rifle leaned against the wall. With gloved right hand less than two inches from curling around the frame.

The whore became just as immobile in her undignified sprawl across the bed. Fisting her hands, screwing her eyes tight shut and clenching her teeth together against the need to vent a vocal response to the searing pain that raced back and forth between its source and her brain.

"You played it right enough to stay alive, Nance," the second man to speak went on.

"I told him nothing and got two broken legs for my trouble," she forced out through her gritted teeth, each word dripping with acid bitterness.

"Come on, Nance. You're always stretching the truth. A little bruised up is all, I figure. Exaggerated somewhat to you, Steele. Even when she was one of our sixteen year old virgins Nance never took a john for more than ten bucks short time!"

"We gonna stand here yakking all night, Lee?"

"No, Chuck. You ready, Steele?"

"For what?" the Virginian asked, nonchalant on the surface but taut inside: prepared to take the chance of reaching those final two inches to grab his rifle.

If the man in the doorway with no trace of a smile on his face even so much as looked like snatching his left hand out from under the right side of his unfastened suit jacket.

The good-humored Lee extended both empty hands forward, turned them over and moved them in a lifting gesture. "To get up on your feet and go meet one of those gentlemen you were asking Nance about. Mr. Ford sent us to bring you to him."

"Dead or alive," Chuck encouraged. "And it'll be the first if you don't take your hand back from close to that rifle."

"Reckon he means it," Steele said to Lee. And dropped his hand to his side.

The smiling man nodded. "Chuck never says anything he doesn't mean. Hear tell you treat that rifle like it's a part of you. If things go against you, I'll see it gets buried alongside you. If things are fine, it'll still be where it is when you come down from seeing Mr. Ford."

The Virginian got to his feet. And moved around the side and end of the bed to go towards the door.

"Hey, you," Nancy called, her voice husky with the strain of containing the vocal release she needed. But as she looked up and screwed her head around to locate the Virginian through her tear-blurred eyes, she managed to unburden herself of a degree of bitterness in the way she scowled at him. "Don't forget your lousy money!"

"Seems to me you earned it, lady," he answered.

"Not for talking, I didn't!" she shot back.

"No. But you're a whore. And you gave me a tumble."

Chapter Seven

The bad-humored Chuck who never took his hand out from inside his coat as he brought up the rear in climbing the stairway to the sixth floor of the Regency Hotel was in his early forties. Short and stocky, with close-cropped brown hair, deep set brown eyes and smoke-tarnished brown teeth. He had a dough-gray, night-time-in-the-city complexion.

Lee, who took the lead during the climb, was a head taller and at least forty pounds heavier. If he carried any excess fat, it did not show in any of the usual places. He had a sun-tanned complexion beneath a head of slicked-down, jet-black hair: this combination of dark colorations serving to emphasize the crystal-clear blueness of his eyes and the gleaming whiteness of his teeth. He was just a couple of years younger than his unsmiling partner.

Both of them were dressed in city suits with vests beneath the jackets. But they wore no ties and their shirts were opened at the throat. Their tastes in colors were conservative—grays and browns at the darker ends of the scale.

As the Virginian was escorted up the carpeted flights of stairs, Lee humming happily to himself and Chuck breathing heavily through his nose, he was tense: expecting around every turn and on each landing to see Powell and Coe. But the ascent to the top floor of the hotel was uneventful.

There were ten suites of rooms up there, the door to number one immediately across the landing from the stairs.

"It's McCoy and Kirby with Adam Steele, Mr. Ford!" Lee called out after rapping his knuckles on the door. He turned the handle and pushed through into the suite without waiting to be invited.

"Wheel him in, Lee!" a man with a gravel-toned voice instructed. "And have laughing boy stick around out there in case those two jokers of Ace's didn't believe what you said."

There was a short, narrow lobby just inside the door from the landing. Then another door, already standing open, which gave on to a large, comfortably furnished living room. Probably, there was too much furniture in the area available. And too much bric-a-brac. All of this of the finest quality whether the material be polished timber, close-woven fabric, hand-cut

108

crystal glass or exquisitely molded porcelain. So that Steele found himself taking great care as he followed Lee's zigzagging course among the tables and chairs across the most unlikely looking hotel room he had ever seen. To guard against knocking over and breaking the wealth of expensive ornaments on display.

"But no rough stuff, Kirby, you hear what I say?" the man added, shouting from the other side of one of the two doors which gave entry to other rooms in the suite.

"Got you, Mr. Ford!" the grim-faced man responded from where he had halted in the inner doorway of the lobby. As he took off his suit jacket and ran a shirt-sleeved arm across his beaded brow.

For the cluttered room was overheated to an uncomfortable degree by the roaring fire in the grate of a large range set into the wall below an ornate, figure-lined mantelshelf. But the bathroom, into which Steele was ushered by the now quiet and impassive Lee McCoy, was much cooler. Although Justin Ford looked warm enough: sitting up to his shoulders in a deep tub of soapy water from which wisps of steam rose as the man moved beneath the surface.

"Evening, sir," the man taking the bath greeted cheerfully through teeth clamped to a cigar and displayed in a grin of what appeared to be genuine warmth.

As the recently dead youngster had accurately reported, Ford was around sixty years old. And he was very thin—the bone structure of his shoulders plain to see under the slack, pale skin and his features extremely angular through the vapor of steam and evil-smelling tobacco smoke which billowed in front of his face. He did, as the boy said, have a curve of gray hair above each ear and a fringe of it at the back of his head. He also had an age-mottled complexion, clear, brown, birdlike eyes under the crinkled hoods of their lids and a great deal of surplus skin hanging in empty sacs from the bones of his cheeks, jaw and throat.

"So you're the young feller Ace Cline reckons can beat me at five card draw, uh?" he continued. And lifted a thin arm out of the water and waved the almost fleshless hand at the end of it towards a chair. "Lee, shift that stuff so that my guest can sit down. And get rid of this for me, will you."

When McCoy turned from taking the robe and heap of towels off the bathroom's only chair, Ford was extending the part-smoked cigar at him. He waved Steele on to the chair, took the cigar and crushed it out in what looked like a solid silver ashtray, and set the stuff from the seat carefully down on the floor. Then he returned to the partially opened door and stood there with arms folded: like a cigar-store Indian.

"I reckon you can afford to buy better information than I can," the Virginain replied, having glanced around to see that, in its own way, the bathroom was as well—and expensively—furnished as the living area of the hotel suite. For the enamelled tub was a fixture, supplied with piped water—that from the faucet marked

HOT presumably heated by the range fire in the main room. One wall was mirrored from floor to ceiling. Against another was a fitment which included a wash basin and several shelves lined with brightly colored bottles and jars. Hot and cold water was also piped to the basin. The floor was carpeted as richly as that in the living room.

"If I have to buy it, I can buy it," Ford said with a shrug of his narrow shoulders. "But on this occasion it was necessary only for laughing boy Chuck Kirby to threaten to blow off Craig Powell's balls. As you no doubt know, sir, wealth and power go hand-in-hand."

"Are you going to tell me how powerful, feller?" Steele asked.

"Be polite!" McCoy growled, and his neutral expression seemed to give added force and meaning to the two words. Just as, the Virginian recalled, Powell could appear far more menacing than Coe without any overt show of hardness.

"Now, Lee," Ford said. "Hopefully, we are dealing here with somebody who has a little more class than Ace's usual run of associates. If your intervention is required, you'll know it."

As he finished speaking, the naked old man in the tub dropped his smile for a moment to glare piercingly at McCoy. And his eyes looked even more birdlike. The tall, sun-tanned man in the doorway compressed his lips as the only hint of the fact that he was hiding resentment at being subtly bawled out in front of a stranger.

First, Steele had been reminded of Powell

111

and Coe in the attitudes and techniques of McCoy and Kirby. Now it was like watching a genuinely cultured, slightly younger but very much thinner version of John C. Cline in the way Justin Ford treated his muscle men.

"I am, Mr. Steele," the man in the tub said, smiling again and his eyes almost warm as they returned to look at the Virginian, "one of the three wealthiest men in Chicago. My main business venture is concerned with the processing and canning of beef. But I am also involved with restaurants, grocery stores and hotels. The Regency, where I am currently living, is now owned by me. I trust you find the hotel to your liking? Of course, in keeping with all my other establishments, it is run on temperance lines. But I understand that, like me, you are not a drinking man. You by choice and me because my stomach will not accept any more hard liquor."

"Is Cline in a competing business?" Steele asked.

"No. Poor Ace is in no business." Ford spoke as if he had genuine sympathy for the man about whom he was talking. "His wealth is inherited from the family business which used to be tailoring. Ace's father and two brothers made an enormous amount of money from supplying uniforms to the Union forces during the war. While Ace was forced to shift the base of his gambling operation from the Mississippi river boats to San Francisco. Much to the pleasure of his father and brothers. Who were hard working men and had no time for Ace. The further away from New York—where they worked—the better as far as the family were concerned.

"Then, in sixty-seven or eight—not too long after the end of the war in any case—one of Ace's brothers took himself a wife. And the wedding feast was held on a boat cruising along one of New York's rivers. The East or the Hudson, I can't remember which it was. But it is of no importance. It was the first time anyone in the Cline family—not including Ace, of course—had ever squandered money on anything that could be termed a luxury. And the last, in the event. Because the steamer sprang a leak and went down. And everyone in the Cline family except Ace was drowned. Not one of them left a will and our mutual friend became a multimillionaire. Robe and towels, Lee."

McCoy jerked forward, responding to the sound of his name much as a well-trained dog might do.

"You want to go and make yourself comfortable in the other room, young feller?" Ford invited. "Take a look around at some of my art possessions, if you've a mind. Understand you come from a fine old Virginian family. So I guess you're a man who can tell what's fine and what's cheap imitation?"

From the way McCoy made a curt gesture with his head, Steele realized that the skinny old man was giving another order rather than making a suggestion. So, with nothing to lose and maybe something to gain, he rose and moved out into the overheated and overcrowded living room. Where he ignored everything—the inanimate collection of high-priced furniture and rich man's trinkets and Chuck Kirby, who was almost equally unmoving except for his deep-set eyes which were never still in their sockets.

Steele sat in a chair as far away from the range as he could get, beyond the velvet-draped window which, he thought, probably looked out over the park and Chicago Harbor to the vast flatness of Lake Michigan beyond. Listening to the sounds from the bathroom which seemed to indicate that McCoy had to lift the thin old man from the tub, towel him dry and then help him into the robe.

As he listened, he watched Kirby put his jacket back on, to conceal the harness which held his shoulder holster in place. And wondered idly if Justin Ford really believed he had fooled his enforced guest into thinking of him as a legitimate businessman.

During this interlude, when Steele unfastened his necktie and unbuttoned his jacket and vest, there was also a whispered conversation in the bathroom. Then came a strange tapping and dragging sound and the Virginian turned his head to see Lee McCoy holding open the door and Justin Ford emerging from the bathroom—needing to walk with the aid of crutches because his left leg was virtually useless. Steele realized the wooden and metal crutches which had horizontal struts into which the old man's elbows and forearms fitted must have been under the washbasin and shelf fitment.

Even with the crutches, Ford made heavy

weather of reaching what was obviously his favorite chair—it was the most used one from the wear on the arms—to the left of the range. His breathing was ragged, sweat stood out on his flaccid face and his eyes were dulled by pain. Until he settled himself gratefully into the chair, gave his crutches to McCoy to lean against the wall, and sighed into a smile.

"Disease with an unpronounceable name, young feller," he said. "It'll kill me soon, but we all have to go some time and I've had a pretty long life already."

He opened the lid of an ivory humidor and took out a large cigar. McCoy lit it for him and then retreated to stand in front of the velvet drapes. As if he thought that Steele, the doorway barred to him by the grim-faced Kirby, might consider escape via the sixth floor window.

"So now you know about Ace and me, Mr. Steele," Ford went on, after drawing in and expelling two clouds of the bad smelling tobacco smoke. "What of you? If Powell is to be believed—and in view of the circumstances in which he spoke to my men, there can be little doubt of that—you were discovered in a small stakes game which got a little out of hand in some drinking establishment down on the south side. You are the best of a not-very-good bunch of players that Powell had been watching ever since his boss agreed to take a chair in the game here tomorrow night."

A clock on the mantel—with a small face surrounded by a tasteless amount of rococo scrollwork—began to chime. Ford waited until the twelfth note had sounded and shook his head. Then smiled. "Tonight, now. Ah, where were we? Oh yes. You were invited to go out and see Ace in that enormous place he's rented on the shore of the lake. Not alone, I'll wager. Does he still prefer the most sluttish looking whores? No matter, that is not of concern to us. You have agreed to play on his behalf because he, poor feller, has lost his nerve since the Boston game. Powell did tell the truth about this, did he not?"

"No reason for him not to have done so," Steele replied evenly.

"Quite so. Now, I do not know what kind of poker player you are, sir. With time so short, poor Ace may have been driven by desperation to hire you." His smile gradually faded and his eyes lost their brightness. Even his voice altered: the gravel tone becoming less pronounced. "But provided there is a half million dollars in front of you—irrespective of whose money it is—you can have a seat at the table. But it's straight game, young feller. Ace never cheated in his life. Then neither did Sam Sinclair and Lowell Banning. Nor me, I suppose I must add. You get my drift, young feller?"

"I was accused of cheating, is all," the Virginian answered.

"Powell said he couldn't be sure. That if you were up to anything, you were better than any sharp he's ever seen. Want you to know that if you get up to anything crooked in the big game, you won't be any better than a lot I've seen. Because I've seen the best. And spotted them for what they were."

He crushed out his cigar. Like the one in the bathroom, finished with before it was a quarter smoked.

"That all?" Steele asked.

"Almost. Lee here saw the shooting in the stable across the alley out back. Because we've had our eye on you ever since you showed up at the hotel with Ace's two jokers tailing you. Now Lee knows that the man with the bum hand killed Roy Dibble—that was the kid with the blond hair—and that Niles Coe and Powell put pay to him. But if we spot you cheating, sir, Lee is liable to tell a different story to the law. Including giving them information as to where he saw a young feller looking much like you drop the two bodies in the lake."

Steele glanced at McCoy and saw that the sun-tanned face was wreathed in a smile again. As he rose from the chair, he said to the good-humored bodyguard. "You can stay happy, feller. You won't have to risk your reputation by telling lies. I play a straight game of poker."

"Sit down again!" Kirby ordered levelly from the doorway where he stood. "Mr. Ford ain't finished yet."

"But very nearly," the thin, crippled old man assured and the Virginian drew a tiny modicum of satisfaction from ignoring what Kirby had said. And remained on his feet. "You see, sir, I do not share your opinion about luck having no part in a game of poker. And in the event that my luck is not at its best during the forthcoming game,

117

you must prove yourself better than the best. Cheat, that is."

"Because you see, Steele," Lee McCoy put in, "Mr. Cline and Mr. Banning and Mr. Sinclair are all as expert as Mr. Ford in spotting when somebody in a game is not playing straight."

"Good old Sam and Lowell will not cause any problems," Ford said. "So I am not asking you to do the impossible, young feller. Just to make sure that, if the cards run for you and not for me, that your backer does not benefit by it."

Ford and McCoy seemed a little disappointed that the Virginian showed no facial response to the proposition which had been put to him. While Ford smiled knowingly and nodded approvingly. Then:

"I can see you possess one of the most important requirements for a first-class card player, young feller," the old man said. "You do not, as they say, wear your heart on your sleeve."

"You through now?" Steele asked.

"Watch your mouth!" Kirby snarled. "I know where your lousy heart is."

"I am all finished, sir," Ford replied to the Virginian. "Except to say that, in this instance, you will do well to bear in mind what Mr. Kirby told you. Up to and during the game, be careful of what you say. Also, I might add, watch your step."

Steele started across the cluttered room, weaving carefully between the scattered, heavily laden furniture.

"And if you wish to know anything else about

118

Ace or myself. Or Lowell or Sam for that matter . . ."

Kirby had made to move out of Steele's path. But he sidestepped back to his sentry position in the doorway as soon as Justin Ford began to speak again. And the Virginian came to an abrupt halt. He did not turn around: instead looked steadily at the gray skinned face of the man who never smiled.

". . . Don't go spreading your money around on kids and whores. You come up and ask me, sir. I'll give you the right information and it won't cost you a thing."

Kirby had to lean to the side to look around the Virginian and see the old man in the chair on the other side of the room.

"All right, laughing boy," Ford instructed and his voice suddenly made him sound bored. "Turn him loose. But keep a tight rein on him. I would not like for him to wander too far away. And lose the opportunity to take that fat cat for every cent he has."

Kirby stepped to one side and gave a jerk of his head to order Steele along the short hallway. Without altering his expression or the way he carried himself, the Virginian went past the scowling man with the deep-set brown eyes, opened the outer door and stepped from the suite on to the landing.

"I'll be down to relieve you in a couple of hours, Chuck!" McCoy called as Kirby followed close behind Steele.

"After I have beaten you again at chess,

119

young feller," Justin Ford put in eagerly. "Bring the table, please."

Steele recalled seeing a finely made table with its top sectioned into brown and cream squares: the black and white porcelain chess pieces aligned in readiness for a game to begin. And as he moved across the landing towards the top of the stairs, he kept this image vivid and firmly fixed in his mind. Which helped him to control the rage that was seething and whirling in his belly: as hot and heavy as molten lead.

When had he started to get angry?

Maybe as far back as early evening when, amid the squalid surroundings of the Broken Promise, Red Wilmot had accused him of cheating. He was many things, a lot of them bad, but a cheat he never had been. At cards or anything else.

He had come out of that poker game only partially satisfied: for the outburst of violence served merely to salve his wounded pride and release some of his anger. Not all, because the act of driving the knife into Wilmot's flesh would have done nothing to erase the suspicion from the minds of those who heard the accusation voiced by the redhaired man.

Steele had always maintained that he cared nothing about what people thought of him. But was this degree of anger he felt now—more intense than he could remember experiencing for many years—a bitter-to-swallow proof that he did care: in one respect, at least?

Certainly he had over-reacted to the only

mildly irritating Craig Powell, which suggested that the supercilious man with the dead-looking green eyes had suffered as much because of the actions of a third party as what he himself did or said.

The killings in the livery stable out back of the hotel? Some more fuel to the flames of the Virginian's anger. As Coe and Powell killed a man in cold blood simply to prevent Steele finding out that Ford was not just in the cannery business. And he let this pass, content for the killers to conceal the mess made by Wilmot and themselves in committing wanton murder. While he tried a new line of approach: pumping the whore to find out about the shady businessman who was the other major player in the scheduled game.

Only to be surprised again. By the more expert, smoother operating McCoy and Kirby. And self-anger was triggered then, as he allowed himself to be made a virtual prisoner and brought up to the opulent surroundings of Justin Ford's luxurious hotel suite. Where, because of the rigid self-control he was exerting, he was forced to listen to instructions that he must cheat at cards or be framed for murder.

But now, as he heard Chuck Kirby close the suite's outer door, the burden of unreleased fury became too much to contain. And Steele altered a forward step into a fast whirl. His right hand going to his neck and then streaking away. Fisted around one weighted corner of the thuggee's scarf.

Kirby was shocked into immobility by the abruptness and speed of the Virginian's transformation. From subservient docility into vicious aggressiveness. He was halfway across the landing between the door and the head of the stairs, an expression of complacent self-satisfaction on his colorless face. Which, in the space of less than a second altered to shock, to fear and then to something which came close to a match for the look which contorted Steele's features.

As the Virginian completed the turn, took a step towards Kirby and then leaned closer: right arm fully extended and the scarf curving out from the gloved hand to go over the man's left shoulder. It was a look which Steele could actually feel tugging at his skin: stretching it so taut that the flesh seemed to be squeezed out from between it and the bone structure beneath. A look which polished the blackness of his eyes to a high sheen, curled back his lips from his teeth like those of a wild animal snarling in a corner and opened wide every pore to drip venom rather than ooze sweat.

"You gotta be—" Kirby started. And delved his left hand under his coat.

As the silken fabric of the scarf curled around the nape of his neck and Steele reached forward with his other gloved hand—fingers hooked to clasp and tightly grip the free swinging weighted corner.

Taken totally unawares by the scarf—Kirby had thought the hurled-forward right fist was a misdirected punch—the man's vicious anger was displaced by a fresh shock as he was jerked off balance by Steele's action of leaning backwards and tugging on both corners of the scarf. And, as his words were caught in his throat, he opened his mouth wider to vent a vocal response to his feelings. But found this was abruptly trapped with the air in his windpipe as the Virginian crossed his hands and forearms and locked his elbows: with the scarf wrapped tightly around Kirby's neck.

Terror replaced shock. And he wrenched his left hand out from where it was caught between his own and the chest of Steele—short of the holstered gun under his right armpit. Then raised it, with the fingers curled like those of his right hand, to try to hook behind the strangling fabric at his throat. But the silk had too close a hold—the flesh bulging out above and below.

And with each part of a second that the stale air was trapped in his lungs, Kirby lost strength: making the prospect of release by his own efforts increasingly more remote.

He had been unbalanced from the moment Steele attained a two-handed grip on the scarf—would have fallen flat out on his face and belly if the Virginian had not stood rock-like in his path. But now, as Kirby's tormentor continued to keep him starved of life-giving air, he did half fall. And Steele allowed the man to drop hard to his knees as the muscles in his legs ceased to function. Then, a moment later, the uselessly clawing hands fell away to thud, palms upwards and fingers splayed, against the carpet beside the folded legs.

In which position Chuck Kirby was in danger

123

of being hanged by the weight of his own stocky body. For Steele, the rage continuing to fill his belly with burning heat and to freeze his features into the expression of ugly viciousness, held the scarf as tightly as ever and allowed his hands and arms to give just a little in relation to his victim's downward movement.

Kirby gazed up at him, brown eyes bulging so that a vast area of white showed around the irises, mouth gaping so wide that the lips looked in danger of splitting open at the corners, and the dough grayness of his skin tone coloring towards purple.

Thus was the man's face and attitude a living—almost dying—tableau of pathetic helplessness. Which served to placate the Virginian's fury by, paradoxically, taunting him with the knowledge that the unfortunate man at his mercy did not deserve to suffer on behalf of everyone else who had contributed to the anger. And Steele saw in his mind's eye another vivid image of the chessboard table top with the expensive pieces on the colored squares.

Chuck Kirby was no more to Justin Ford than one of those porcelain models. And was being used by the puny old man to try to mold Steele into another such piece. Wilmot, too, had tried to manipulate the Virginian to serve his own purpose. While John C. Cline sought to buy him into making the moves he wanted.

All of which was all right if the people concerned had simply come out and said what they wanted: instead of which they had all tried to use fear or force to gain the respective objectives. Which had taken cumulative effect on Steele. As a result of which Kirby—who happened to be in the wrong place at the right time—was taken to within a few seconds of losing his life before the Virginian realized what little he had to gain by killing the man. A fleeting moment of triumph and satisfaction, such as he might gain from successfully swatting a fly which was irritating him: in the full knowledge that as soon as he opened the screen door, a whole bunch of others would swarm inside.

He closed his lips over his teeth, pursed them to allow a low whistle to escape, and unclasped his gloved hands. On the verge of unconsciousness, Kirby was aware enough of what was happening to him to vent a grunt of relief with the stale breath before he sucked in gratefully on the fresh air. And his eyes as they started to close expressed a boundless gratitude.

But then Steele, as he stepped back from the man, brought up a knee: which smashed hard into the face of the falling forward Kirby. Which flipped him to the side and then into a roll on to his back: leaving him spreadeagled across the landing, his eyes fastened shut, his face dough-gray again, and with crimson ooze spilling down his jaw from where teeth had bitten into his lower lip.

The Virginian's breathing was more forced than that of the unconscious man: as he draped the damaging scarf back around his neck and tried to convince himself he had done the right thing. At the same time he struggled to squeeze out of himself the remnants of the hot anger.

125

He did not know how long it took to do this. Which, after it was achieved, was a cause for anxiety. For a man in the grip of such an all-engulfing emotion had his alertness impaired and his defenses down: and was thus an easy target for anyone who wished him harm. This was the lesson he had learned way back in the War Between the States. The one which had been concerning him recently. And yet he had allowed his temper to flare.

His own breathing became regular and less noisy: and so he heard the ragged, wheezing sounds made by the man sprawled on the floor. He looked up from Kirby and rapidly swung his head from side to side and then back to look over his shoulder.

The landing and the stairway were deserted. The doors, including that to Ford's suite, remained firmly closed. Outside the hotel the wind off the lake continued to whine and moan. Inside, only the sounds of the unconscious man's involuntary labored breathing broke the otherwise total silence.

Until Steele moved, stooping, taking hold of an arm and a leg of Kirby and hauling him up on his right shoulder. He rested for a moment, then came erect.

Despite Kirby's lack of height, the man was no lightweight. So the Virginian wasted no time in moving across to the entrance of suite one, turning the handle and using the rump of the unconscious man to swing the door wide. It banged hard against the hallway wall so that both Justin Ford and Lee McCoy had early warning that something was wrong. And were looking up with a mixture of surprise and fear at the open inner doorway when Steele stepped on to the threshold, Chuck Kirby draped precariously across his shoulder.

Ford was still in his well-used chair, while McCoy had drawn forward another seat, the chessboard table between their knees.

The old man recovered his composure quickly, while the younger one was still in the process of developing anger while his eyes raked Steele for sight of an overt weapon. Ford was content to concentrate his steady gaze on the Virginian's face.

"Don't do anything you might later regret, Lee!" he said sharply. Then moderated his tone to add: "As this young feller appears to have done."

Steele shook his head. "You should never judge by appearances."

"I don't. Experience is my basis. And I know that if you have a choice between killing a man like Kirby and making an enemy of him, it is best to kill him. So you made a bad mistake, sir. He will come after you and not be satisfied until he has more than evened the score with you."

The Virginian used both hands and his shoulder to power a forward motion—hurling the considerable weight of Kirby's lax form several feet into the room. Flailing arms and trailing legs knocked several ornaments to the floor. Then the entire bulk of the unfeeling man came down hard on a table with spindly legs. And the sound of splintering wood and smashing glass and china almost masked the duller thud of flesh against carpet.

"Could be," Steele replied when the clamor had ended. "Nobody's perfect. But try not to make the same mistake twice."

As he spoke, he saw cracks in the veneer of calmness which the frail old man had drawn about himself. Through the cracks, a deep anxiety showed.

"What do you intend to do?"

"Beat it out of town if he had any sense!" McCoy rasped.

"Get some rest and play some cards."

Ford blinked and his tongue darted out to lick the thin, dry lips. "You mean the big game?"

"Sure."

"You have to be crazy, Steele!" McCoy snarled. And then looked pointedly at the ugly clock in the center of the mantelshelf. "That game in the Illinois Room doesn't start until eight o'clock. That's almost twenty hours away from now. If you think you can hide all that time and then show up and—"

"Mr. Steele will not need to hide, Lee," Justin Ford interrupted, as the last of the cracks were patched over. "He is no fool. I badly misjudged him. He did not do the same with me. Without somebody representing Ace Cline at the table, there can be no big game. I will see you at eight, young feller. And you have my word that no harm will come to you as a result of what I say or do."

·Steele smiled. "At least until the end of the game."

A nod.

"But, Mr. Ford—"

"Mr. Steele has exhibited his resentment of our methods, Lee," the crippled old man explained. "Much to the dismay, very shortly, of poor Chuck. But he remains firmly over the barrel of what occurred in the livery stable earlier."

"So he's lying. He'll beat it out of town and—"

"In that unlikely event, my guarantee is, of course, null and void. That is understood, is it not, Mr. Steele?"

"I reckon we've reached an understanding, feller," the Virginian drawled. "Anybody makes any more mistakes, they'll be rubbed out."

Chapter Eight

Steele slept in room 101 with the chair propped under the handle of the door and the emptied water pitcher from the bureau tied to the bottom of the drape curtains at the window. Neither precaution would prevent anybody entering his room: but they would cause an intruder to make a great deal of noise in gaining entry. He slept beneath the covers, stripped to his longjohns. And shared the comfort with his Colt Hartford, his right hand fisted around the frame of the rifle. He did not sleep deeply, but he slept soundly. In a bed with a roof over his head for the first time since he left San Francisco.

He dreamed of that far-off city and of Renita who had been a whore. No better than Laverne

131

or Nancy. But a lot more appealing to a lonesome man. Alive.

The Virginian came awake abruptly, was laggard in tightening his grip around the rifle and in recalling where he was and why he was there. This took all of a second or maybe as many as two. Which was as unusual for him as dreaming. And allowing the hot rage of mindless temper to take control of his actions.

An image of the face of the Mexican whore was still firmly fixed against the retinas of his eyes as they opened and flicked from side to side in the sockets: seeking to recognize something in the dimly lit surroundings which would trigger a memory from the more recent past. Renita was smiling. Then there was blood on her face. And death in her eyes. Steele's own vision blurred and the memories he was seeking crowded into his troubled mind.

The light was that of morning on a gray Chicago day, creeping into a room of the Regency Hotel on Michigan Avenue, under and around the curtains draped at the window. And he had been let off the hook. For no one had taken advantage of his uncharacteristic lapse of concentration on the present as he woke from a sleep during which his sixth sense for impending danger had obviously not been operating.

So he was able to release his hold on the Colt Hartford and use both hands to fist the grit of sleep from his eyes: ignoring the slight dampness on his knuckles. As he got out of the bed, shuddered under the assault of the cold air and went to the window to draw the drapes apart.

The wind and the rain had stopped but the sky above the sprawling city was as ominously low and gray as it had been yesterday morning. The holes which the gusting night wind had torn in the clouds had been repaired and there was not a sign of movement in any part of the sky visible from the window at the rear of the hotel. Lower, the jagged skyline of Chicago was smudged here and there by woodsmoke from chimneys. Lower still, the pools in the broken surface of the alley between the hotel and the livery stable looked as large and as deep as last night. Standing down at the far end of the alley, where he could watch every window at the rear of the Regency, was Niles Coe. He was warmly dressed to the extent that it was not possible to see in any detail his face or the way he held himself. But as he pushed away from where he had been leaning against a wall and began to pace back and forth across the mouth of the alley, his shoulders hunched and his hands thrust deep into coat pockets, Coe gave the impression of being cold, damp, dejected and ready to get angry on the slightest pretext.

Recalling what had happened to him on the landing of the sixth floor a few hours ago, Steele could have sympathized a little with how the powerfully built gunman was feeling. But he didn't, as he washed up and shaved in the cold water which last night he had tipped from the pitcher into the bowl on the bureau: for he found himself thinking, enviously, of the luxuries which Justin Ford enjoyed. Not least of which was running hot water.

Then, as he dressed, the Virginian chided himself for giving free rein to his mind to conjure up such futile thoughts. Dreams and the initial images he saw during the moments of waking were something over which he could not exercise control. But when he was fully awake and totally aware of himself and his environment? Occasionally, in quiet times when there was nothing more urgent to occupy him, he allowed his mind to bring forward and dust off recollections of the comforts and luxuries he had once enjoyed. But never did he indulge in self-pity: which was an emotion akin to envy.

He was who he was and what he was as a result of his own actions. And because of this if he could eat well, sleep warm, dress decently and keep clean it was the most he could expect. Anything more than this was cream in his coffee or butter on his sourdough bread. And it was not in his nature to covet the lifestyles or possessions of other men—or it never had been until today.

Grimacing his response to the bad start to the day, he removed the pitcher from the curtains, took the chair out from under the door handle and left the room. He carried his rifle, his saddlebags and his bedroll with the sheepskin coat lashed to it.

The lobby was as underused as it had been last night. Ruddy was still behind the desk, and was gripped by fear midway through a wide yawn when he saw the Virginian descending the stairs. As the interrupted yawn developed into a fit of coughing, the desk clerk trying to dislodge the sudden tension from his throat, the second occupant of the lobby showed himself.

Nancy La Salle had gone to wherever whores go to sleep alone in the day time and the chair she had occupied last night was now filled by Lee McCoy. Who showed not a trace of the easy-going nature he had pretended to have before his partner caught the brunt of Steele's hot anger. Today his sun bronzed face was set in an expression of vicious enmity as he turned in the chair to look towards Steele, then unfolded fast to his feet. His right hand was thrust into the side pocket of his suit jacket.

"You're not leaving, mister!" His tone, his expression and the way he turned to face the Virginian—so that he could aim the small gun in his pocket at him—combined to emphasize that it was a clear order rather than a surprised enquiry.

"You're right, feller," Steele replied evenly as he reached the desk where Ruddy had cleared the constriction from his throat but continued to show a great deal of anxiety in his deep set eyes. "But neither am I going to pay another day's room rent just to store my gear. I'll settle for the one night. And be grateful if the hotel will take care of this stuff until I'm ready to leave Chicago."

He had not looked at McCoy as he spoke. Now he placed his saddlebags and bulky bedroll on the desktop and gazed inquiringly at Ruddy. Who in turn glanced towards McCoy,

135

received an instruction by gesture and smiled his relief that the decision had been taken by somebody else.

"Five dollars, sir. And the hotel will be happy to take care of your possessions. But you really should take your coat, Mr. Steele. It's very cold out."

"One day Ruddy'll make some kid a fine mother," McCoy said and he sounded as relieved as the desk clerk looked. Now that the Virginian had made it plain he did not intend to renege on what he agreed to do.

"If you have a restaurant in the hotel, I have no need to go out," Steele told Ruddy as he handed him a five-dollar bill. And turned away from the desk to see that Lee McCoy was showing his easy-going smile. Without any visible sign of strain.

"Through the doors to the right, Mr. Steele," Ruddy supplied eagerly, anxious to be of service. "Breakfast'll be getting started pretty soon now."

He screwed his head around to look up at the clock on the wall above the desk, which showed the time as 7.30.

"You make a deal with Cline's men, feller?" Steele asked as he dropped into a chair close to where McCoy sat but with his back to him: facing towards the hotel entrance but with the restaurant doorway in view, also. He rested the Colt Hartford across the arms of the chair.

"You lost me," McCoy growled, puzzled.

"You're covering the front. Niles Coe is watching the rear. Because this is Ford terri-

136

tory, you get to draw the warmest picket post?"

"Never knew that muttonhead was out there. We didn't cover the back of the hotel because Mr. Ford didn't figure it was your style to sneak away. Looks like he was absolutely right, doesn't it?"

"Nobody's wrong all the time."

"Wrong to think you'd hold still for Chuck Kirby to ride close herd on you?"

"That, too," the Virginian responded. "But it seems to me your boss made a more expensive mistake when he bought this hotel." He glanced across at the desk and caught Ruddy at the start of a yawn this time. "I reckon the whore was joking last night when she said she wanted you to wake her when the rush hour started?"

Ruddy grimaced. "The kind of joke nobody laughs at, sir."

"Mr. Ford is happy," McCoy added, without enthusiasm. Then lowered his voice and leaned sideways from his chair to get closer to Steele. "But not so happy as he was before you threw Chuck on to that table. That was a Chippendale. Old and worth a lot of money. And you smashed up some pretty good Philadelphia porcelain as well. If the game doesn't end up the way Mr. Ford wants, he'll take into account what you did last night."

"Did I hurt Kirby much?"

"Just his pride. And Mr. Ford wasn't wrong about that. Been safer for you if you'd killed Chuck."

"But I don't have to keep looking over my shoulder? At least not until after the game?"

137

"That's right, Steele. Chuck's not too bright but he knows enough not to disobey Mr. Ford's orders. But if you don't get that smart by tonight, Chuck'll really enjoy doing what he's told."

McCoy vented a short, brittle laugh. As the two unmarked doors in a side wall of the lobby were folded inwards to reveal a section of clean-looking restaurant featured by neatly laid tables. These tables covered with white linen cloths and set with good quality cutlery. The girl who opened up the place wore a black dress, white apron and white cap. She was young, Mexican and unattractive. The smile she raised for Steele and McCoy as they entered the restaurant took a great deal of effort.

"Two together?" she asked.

"Why not?" McCoy asked Steele.

"I'm not proud," the Virginian replied.

Steele chose the table by one of the four windows, hung with net curtains, which offered a view of bustling Michigan Avenue. He ordered a full ham-and-eggs breakfast while McCoy wanted just coffee. Ford's man seemed surprised when, after resting the Colt Hartford against the window sill, Steele did not take off his hat and gloves. After the sullen-faced Mexican girl had delivered a coffee pot and two cups, McCoy said:

"You dress city style, you talk southern but you're as western as chaparral and sagebrush, aren't you?"

Steele poured himself a cup of coffee and set down the pot. "That bother you?"

"What you're doing in Chicago bothers me."
He had to use a handkerchief around the coffee
pot handle to keep from burning his palm and
fingers.

"It was at the end of the trail I was riding. If
I had kept on going my horse and me would
have gotten pretty wet in the lake."

"And it was just good fortune that you happened to reach town in time for the big game?"

Steele pursed his lips and shifted his piceous
eyes away from the dreary view through the
window to look directly into McCoy's face. But
waited until his breakfast had been set down in
front of him before he asked:

"Would you like to get straight to the point,
feller? If you don't want to—"

"It's all too convenient, Steele," McCoy put
in. "A guy like you showing up at this particular
time. To play for Cline. You have to be a good
player. Better than good. What I think you are
is a professional, mister. A pro Cline knew from
when he was working out in California. Or
maybe when he was operating on the Mississippi riverboats, you coming from the south.
Am I right?"

"Paid for my room and intend to pay for this
food with money I won in a poker game, feller.
Reckon you could say that the last card game I
was in, I was playing for a living. But I do lots
of other things beside play cards. When I need
to make money."

McCoy had not shown his smile since coming
into the restaurant. Until now, his evenly
tanned features and amazingly clear blue eyes

139

had been expressing eager attentiveness. Abruptly, this was displaced by anxiety.

"Look, Steele. How much would you take to get astride your saddle and ride out of this city?"

The Virginian revealed his surprise only in the way that, for a moment, he paused in the act of raising a food-laden fork from the plate to his mouth. There was silence in the restaurant while he chewed then swallowed the food.

"How much you reckon your boss is worth, feller?"

"Don't be crazy, Steele. That's—"

"How much?"

"I have no idea. But be realistic. If you'll—"

"Find out. In cash, real-estate values, company stocks. I'll leave the city for eleven per cent of the total."

"You're out of your mind!" McCoy said huskily.

"One per cent above what Cline has offered me to take his chair in the game."

"If you win!"

The Virginian shrugged his shoulders. "That's right, feller. But with nothing to lose, I'm willing to take the chance. And because of there being no risk to me, I only pitched my price to you at one per cent above Cline's offer."

McCoy suddenly looked venomously hate-filled as he had last night when Steele re-entered Ford's suite with Chuck Kirby over his shoulder. "No risk to you, you crazy fool?" he snarled, keeping his voice low so that the plain-faced Mexican girl waiting beside the kitchen doorway could not hear the words. "Last night we could have finished you like that!" He snapped his fingers and thumb. "And if you win money tonight, you lose your life. You better believe that, mister!"

He hooked his hands over the edge of the table and started to rise to his feet. But he was only a couple of inches up from the chair when the window glass shattered—to shower a million razor-sharp shards across the table and at the two men.

McCoy hurled himself to the side, a strangled cry of pain and alarm bursting from his throat. And beads of blood erupting from the side of his face.

While Steele, starting his move a fraction of a second earlier, powered backwards: using his feet against the floor and his back against the back of the chair to gain purchase and speed.

And the homely faced Mexican girl gasped, looked down at where the black dress contoured her left breast, saw the wet stain expanding around the hole in the fabric, raised a hand to touch her fingertips to the stickiness. Then saw the color of her own blood and screamed.

She was the last of the three to sprawl to the floor. Dead from a bullet in her heart.

When the Virginian had started to force himself backwards from the table, dropped his fork and reached with both hands for his rifle, his actions were triggered by an instinct for danger rather than any clear sign that it threatened. It

141

was just that, on the periphery of his vision, he saw an abrupt flurry of fast movement out on Michigan Avenue. He tensed himself for action then. As he shifted his gaze away from McCoy's angry face to get a more distinct impression of what caused the commotion. And it was then that he erupted into action. When he saw three riders spurring their mounts up off the avenue and on to the sidewalk. Emerging from the thick traffic to send the pedestrians scurrying and leaping from their path. This twenty feet short of where Steele and McCoy sat by the window.

He received no lasting impression of the men or their horses. Did not even see any of them reach for guns. And no longer had them in sight when he saw the window shatter, heard the triple report of three revolvers fired in unison, felt pinpricks of pain against the backs of his hands.

Then came a greater, jarring pain as the back of his head hit the floor and his whole body was juddered by the impact of the chair coming to rest. By that time he had his rifle gripped two handed and the hammer cocked. He glimpsed the Mexican girl collapsing to the floor and knew from the dulling of her eyes that she was dead. He heard Lee McCoy cursing, the man's growling tones counterpointing the sounds of traffic and shouting which the bitterly cold airstream carried through the opening of the shattered window. Just for a very short time it was possible to hear, also, the clatter of galloping hoofbeats against the asphalt sidewalk.

But this sound was gone before the Virginian started to get to his feet. And the trio of horses and their riders were no longer in sight when he was in a position to peer out through the window. His appearance there, with the Colt Hartford angled across the front of his chest, triggered more fearful hurry and frightened sounds from the shocked people who saw him. And he withdrew from the window, so that the net curtains fell back into place.

"Oh, my God, what happened?" Ruddy shrieked as he ran into the restaurant and pulled up short, his gaze shifting from Steele who had blood on the backs of his gloved hands, to McCoy whose face on one side dripped crimson and then located the utterly unmoving Mexican girl—who was slumped on her belly, hiding the fatal wound. "Carmelita! Is she . . . ?"

"No, feller," the Virginian rasped through clenched teeth. "She's dead. Now she was."

Chapter Nine

Justin Ford had the money-based power to get things done. Also to have not done other things which would be done automatically if such a man with such influence were not involved. And so it was that the death of Carmelita Rosa was investigated by the Chicago police as a crime of passion: with the prospect of it becoming a very long case. For, despite her homeliness, the Mexican girl had a lot of lovers. Or so the detective who questioned Steele maintained. The fat, dull-eyed, untidily dressed lawman with bad breath did not question Lee McCoy who claimed to have seen nothing until the three bullets shattered the window. And, as soon as it was learned that murder had resulted from the shooting, none of the witnesses on the street waited around to talk with the police.

Which meant there was just Steele alone who claimed that three horsemen had galloped along the sidewalk and fired their revolvers into the Regency Hotel window. And this did not match up with the lawman's preconceived theory about a jealous lover being responsible for the killing. An idea which the man must have got when—before he even came to take a look at the scene of the crime—he was summoned by Ruddy to visit the suite of Justin Ford.

Such was the power of the elderly cripple. He could pervert the course of justice. He could also get a shattered window replaced, a bloodstained floor cleaned and a bullet-scarred wall repaired even before the investigating officer had finished questioning the only available eyewitness.

"I'll bear in mind what you told me, mister," the detective muttered sourly as he made to leave the lobby where the question and answer session had taken place. "But it all happened so fast, didn't it? The window got busted and cold air hit you in the eyes. And there was all that flyin' glass that cut up Mr. McCoy's face so bad. Only natural a man should shut his eyes real tight in that kinda mess. And then there was the curtains between you and the street. I ain't sayin' you ain't sure you didn't see three men. I'm just sayin' you could've been mistaken. Thanks for your time, anyway. You enjoy the rest of your stay in our fair city, all right?"

The Virginian grimaced and was on the point of making some comment about the man's use of the term "fair city." But the detective had already turned around to go towards the doorway which gave on to the street. And he realized the futility of objecting to what was happening. He had absolutely no interest in the unfortunate Mexican girl who was now on her way to the city morgue. While the venal or frightened lawman had no interest in the intended victim—be it Steele or McCoy. And if the volley of gunfire had been meant to tear into the flesh of the Virginian . . . well, it had never been in his nature to let the law take care of his troubles. Especially not corrupt representatives of the law. Be it in a hot and dusty one-street western town or a bleak and blustery sprawling eastern city.

So Steele let the detective go without further talk and for the remainder of the day took precautions against further attempts on his life. For most of this time, he sat in the lobby with the rifle resting across the arms of his chair. But with the chair against the wall beside the desk now: from which position he could see anyone who came in—be it through the street entrance, down the stairs, out of the restaurant or by way of any of the doors which were marked STAFF ONLY or gave on to the hotel's public rooms.

Soon after the lawman left, a bleary-eyed old-timer in his seventies appeared from the staff accommodation to take over from Ruddy as the day desk clerk. He showed Steele a toothless grin, received a curt nod in response and decided to leave the exchange at that. Ruddy went through the door the old man had left

147

open and did not even glance at Steele. At noon, Nancy La Salle emerged through the same doorway under the stairs. Dressed in the same style black and white as Carmelita Rosa that morning. The whore was obviously not happy in her new, probably enforced role. She limped, as if her fall of the previous night still caused pain.

And she did her waitressing chore with ill humor and bad grace when, at one o'clock, Steele entered the restaurant to eat lunch. He sat at a table, his back to the wall again, out of direct line with any of the windows: and ordered steak and fresh vegetables without receiving any kind of acknowledgement from the woman. She did not, in fact, speak until he asked for the check.

"You have to pay for the breakfast as well, Steele. I hear you overlooked that in all the excitement this morning."

"Sure, lady," he said, giving her a five. "The Regency looks in need of every cent it's owed."

"It ain't usually like this."

"Why now?"

"The card game, of course. No reservations were taken beyond yesterday. With at least two million cash goin' to be on the table in the Illinois Room tonight, who wants a hotel full of strangers around?"

"Keep the change," Steele said as he rose from the table.

She looked at what the cook scrawled on the check and pulled a face as she snapped: "Big spender, ain't you, Steele? Twenty-five cents is—"

"Something to help you keep up with the cost of living, lady," he cut in evenly. "The Mexican girl died for nothing."

The afternoon dragged by as uneventfully as the morning following the departure of the detective. Because it was Sunday, the broad width of Michigan Avenue visible through the glazed sections of the hotel's entrance doors became less crowded. No one who strolled by the doorway made any attempt to approach the liveried doorman who stood in the porch—unmoving even when the wind started to blow off the lake again. And no horseman or carriage driver slowed down in the vicinity of the Regency. With dusk came more rain and the doorman draped a waterproof cape around his shoulders. As the old timer came out from behind the desk to light the lobby's lamps.

"Looks to be set for another bad night, sir," he said. Then added quickly: "Far as the weather goes, that is."

Steele nodded absently and continued to remain actively alert while appearing to be totally relaxed. Watching for the first sign of new danger as his mind examined a whole host of reasons why this should be necessary.

Just as, at the start of his day's stint behind the desk, the old man had been discouraged from conversation with Steele by the Virginian's churlish acknowledgement to an opening, so it was again. But this time the old timer did mumble, as he returned behind the desk:

"Whatever's ailing you, weren't my fault. So why the hell—"

"You know who's fault it is, feller?" Steele interrupted.

The man was surprised his soft-spoken remarks had been overheard. "What's that, sir?"

"You know why somebody tried to kill me this morning?"

"You? Way I heard it, it was one of the Mex girl's boyfriends killed her. A fit of jealousy."

"Exactly that, Mr. Troy," Ruddy said as he entered the lobby to take over the desk for the night. Looking well-rested and freshly washed up and shaved. Wearing the same suit as last night, but with a clean shirt. He took a fob watch from his vest pocket and checked it with the clock on the wall above the desk. And his nod seemed to indicate that the watch time matched that of the clock. Which was seven. Then Nancy La Salle, who had not emerged from the restaurant before, pushed open the doors and looked balefully at the three men in the lobby.

"You should eat right away if you intend to eat at all, Mr. Steele," Ruddy advised, much more self-confident now than he had been this morning or last night. "If you are late starting the game, Mr. Ford will not like it."

"And when Mr. Ford doesn't like something, feller?" Steele asked as he got to his feet and canted the Colt Hartford to his shoulder.

"Pardon?" Ruddy asked, flipping open the register from habit, raking his eyes down the blank columns and then closing it.

Troy, the old timer, hurried to go through the doorway and closed the door behind him. As Nancy La Salle retreated into the restaurant.

"He may own you, feller," the Virginian said, and pointed to one side of the lobby then the other. "And him. And her. And McCoy and Kirby. The biggest canning business in the city. Even the local law here in Chicago. Just for the record, if he needs me and I'm late, he has to wait."

Ruddy's new found composure wilted like a candle set down too near a stove. And Steele immediately regretted his sour-toned attack on the man and the others who were in the power of the aged, despotic cripple who lived in such abundant luxury on the top floor of the hotel. For he was a stranger in this strange world of the city of Chicago. With no way of knowing how many compromises a man—or a woman— had to make in order to eat, drink, sleep and work at a level far enough above that of degradation so that their existence was not tainted by the stench of their own living.

That they were as corrupt as the tyrant who ruled them? Because by compliance they contributed to the rottenness? No, for they were not free to choose. Because they were too weak to break away and attain freedom? But weakness was to be pitied, not attacked. Unless by a man incapable of pity. Who might regret what he did—fleetingly—but feel justified in using strength against weakness if there was good enough reason for doing so.

And to Steele's mind there was no better reason for doing anything than the simple clear-cut one of staying alive.

Ruddy became progressively more afraid as the Virginian crossed the lobby towards him. Then actually vented a short gasp of terror and had to bite down on his lower lip to keep from trembling when the barrel of the Colt Hartford was slapped to rest on the closed register: its muzzle less than six inches away from a button of the man's vest.

"I know about his legitimate business interests," Steele said. "How else does Ford make money?"

There was a lamp on each end of the desk, both of them throwing up light into his face so that the clerk could see every feature plainly. Including the eyes, as black as pitch and as expressionless as damp and shiny pebbles.

"What?" A hard swallow. "Pardon?"

"Reckon the whore you do your double act with must have told you I've been asking questions that get folks into trouble. But we're alone here. No one around to give you a bad time. Except me."

"I don't know what you are talking about, Mr. Steele!" Ruddy protested. And his Adam's apple bobbed up and down as the words were squeezed out around it.

Then it stopped working. And his entire being became frozen into rigidity as he heard the hammer of the Colt Hartford click back.

"Lots of people want me to play cards with Justin Ford tonight," Steele said softly. "But I get the impression I'll be getting into more than just a poker game. Especially after, when he couldn't pay me to get out of Chicago, Lee McCoy had a bunch of gunman try to kill me. As a result of which an innocent Mexican girl died. From a badly aimed revolver bullet. Who cared, Ruddy? Nobody. The same nobody who'll cry buckets if you should die. From a perfectly aimed rifle bullet."

He pushed the rifle forward a few inches and Ruddy seemed unable to shift his feet. He merely sucked in has flat belly.

"Tell him, Ruddy," Nancy La Salle rasped from the restaurant doorway. "What does it matter? He will play anyhow."

The thin man behind the desk was vastly relieved that he had received advice. He tugged at the sides of his suit jacket, ran the fingers of one hand through his hair and licked beads of sweat off the flesh above his top lip. "Mr. Ford is in the prostitution business, sir. It is his intention to expand into other similar fields. Advised by Mr. McCoy who knows about such things. This is the rumor we hear, anyway. We understand, too, that Mr. McCoy is afraid you will beat Mr. Ford at poker. Take him for everything he has which would not—"

"Grateful to you, Ruddy," Steele said as he canted the Colt Hartford to his shoulder. He looked towards the restaurant entrance, but the whore-cum-waitress had gone from sight. "Which door leads to the Illinois Room?"

The thin man pointed across the lobby to a

pair of doors, a match for those to the restaurant and directly opposite them. At the foot of the stairs and unmarked. "Those, sir."

"Are they locked?"

"But of course, sir!" He had himself sufficiently under control to be able to be shocked by the question. "With such a high-stakes card game due to take place, no one has been allowed inside since it was prepared for tonight's event. Under the personal supervision of Mr. Justin Ford himself."

Steele nodded and crooked a finger. "Come with me, Ruddy?"

"Sir?"

"Just do it."

His nervousness starting to build again, the clerk with the corpse-like face came out from behind the desk and walked alongside the Virginian. Around the scattering of chairs and tables and cuspidors to the pair of doors he had pointed out. Then:

"Oh, no!" he gasped. As Steele raised a leg and lashed out so that the underside of his boot cracked into the painted timber between the door handles. And the doors sprang open. With enough momentum to bang against the walls inside the room.

"I reckoned Ford kept the key, Ruddy?"

A nod. As Nancy La Salle appeared in the doorway of the restaurant, curious to find out the reason for the noise.

Steele made a gesture with his head to her. "More witnesses the better, lady."

"What?"

"Ford seems to be some kind of tin god around here," Steele answered, sharing his again impassive expression between the anxious whore and the agitated desk clerk. "It may be that where cards are concerned, he's as far above reproach as the real one in all things. But I'd still like to check over this room. With witnesses to check that I don't get up to anything I shouldn't."

"Feel free to do so, sir," the gravel voice of Justin Ford invited from the landing at the top of the stairs.

All those in the lobby swung their heads to look up at the speaker. And saw the emaciated old man standing there on his crutches. With McCoy on one side of him and Kirby on the other, both the younger men showing signs of the facial injuries they had received. Kirby had a swollen and scabbed lower lip while the left side of McCoy's face was a mass of ugly red ridges where the countless cuts had bled and were now starting to heal. Both of them glowered while the man between them smiled superciliously.

"Although why you should distrust me after I have told you of my plan, I cannot think, young man." He started to come down the stairs, using the crutches with great difficulty.

"You foresaw the killings in the livery?" the Virginian asked pointedly.

"Something else would have occurred," Ford replied offhandedly, after he had reached the foot of the stairs. "Come, Ruddy. Light the lamps in the Illinois Room so that our friend may do whatever it is he feels he must do."

The desk clerk was totally at ease again. Now that it was necessary only to comply with orders from the man who paid him. And the whore, who had started to cross the lobby, looked relieved as she turned and went back into the restaurant.

"Incidentally, young feller," Ford went on, as cheerfully as before, as McCoy and Kirby took up positions to either side of him again. "I was very pleased to hear that you did not suffer any grave injury as a result of the most unfortunate shooting incident this morning."

"Reckoned you would be," Steele replied wryly as he moved into the Illinois Room where the darkness was being driven back into corners by the lamps Ruddy lit.

Ford laughed. "Of course, sir. Here am I making polite conversation. When I know full well you think me a hypocrite if I pretended to be concerned for your health for any but selfish reasons. One hundred thousand."

Steele halted just inside the room and turned to look back at the man on the crutches. "Reasons or dollars?" he asked.

Another laugh. "Both, perhaps. I made you an offer of freedom from prosecution on a double murder charge if you prevented Ace Cline from winning tonight. Upon reflection, I feel this is an entirely negative approach. So I have therefore decided to increase my bid—for your services, shall we say?—by one hundred thousand dollars. One large or a great many small reasons for you to cooperate with me. And, needless to say, should the cards not run for you and I win by default, as it were, I will have no way of knowing this. So you will be paid, nonetheless. Unless you are one of those strange people who place honor above material gain? In which case you would doubtless tell me the truth and refuse the reward."

His laughter went on for longer this time. And its tone was derisory.

"Long time since I did that, feller," Steele drawled.

"So you're gonna do what Mr. Ford tells you, mister?" Chuck Kirby growled, the slight movement of his jaw necessary to speak obviously erupting pain in his punctured and bruised lower lip. He had never looked less like smiling.

"Now, now, laughing boy," Ford chided. "Don't try to tax your brain with thoughts. Of course the young feller must do what I ask. Or be charged with murder." The old man suddenly abandoned any pretense of treating the matter lightly. To gaze down from his height advantage with a look of such power in his eyes that it served to set aside the fact that he was old and thin and lame. "For has he not already seen today that a man as rich as I gets to have much more than mere money in his pocket?"

"From patrolman up to the feller at the top?" Steele posed. "Nobody's that rich, Ford."

"You are inexperienced in the ways of the city, young feller. Some key men in key posts is all it takes." Another short laugh, of pure enjoyment. "Yes, I suppose you could say I have quite a few key men in my pocket, Mr. Steele."

The Virginian pursed his lips. "From what I've seen, the worst bunch money can buy, feller."

Chapter Ten

The Illinois Room of the Regency Hotel was large enough to stage a small ball and small enough to provide the setting for a big money poker game. It was about a hundred feet long by thirty wide with panelled walls on which hung a series of gilt-framed oil paintings of mid-western landscapes. The four tall windows which faced Michigan Avenue were hung with heavy velvet drapes, green in color. The floor was polished hardwood, marked by countless scuff marks. The ceiling was decorated with rococo moldings, dirty white with the stains of rising tobacco smoke. There was a bare board stage at the far end of the room and along the side opposite the curtained windows was a line of encircled tables. There were a dozen lamps with ornate shades fixed to wall brackets. Plus a group of six other lamps hung chandelier fashion from the center of the ceiling. A table, larger than the ones along the wall, was positioned immediately beneath this central group of lamps. It was covered with green baize and had four chairs around it.

As Steele strolled around the room, satisfying himself that it contained no inherent aids to cheating, Ruddy lit two lamps on each of the side walls, then used a rope to lower the chandelier cluster so that he could light these as well. Thus, when the man with the death-mask face had hauled on the rope and tied it in place, a pool of very bright lamplight coned down on to the table: and enough spilled outwards to supplement the glowing wall fixture and adequately illuminate every corner of the room.

"You are happy with the arrangements I have made, young feller?" Justin Ford called from where he stood on his crutches in the open doorway, flanked by McCoy and Kirby.

The Virginian stepped down off the stage after checking a door which led off to one side—it was locked and the key was in the lock on this side.

"Reckon it beats the Broken Promise Saloon," Steele answered.

"Ah, the place where your talent was recognized," the old man responded.

"It was a small game with old cards," the Virginian drawled as he approached the table, his boot heels rapping on the hardwood floor. "Guess you'll have sealed decks? All right if I sit here?"

He came to a halt and rested his free hand on the back of the chair which faced the lobby doorway.

"The first man to the table has the pick of the seats, sir," Ford said and started forward. The effort of using the crutches was beginning to tell and he breathed heavily and did not speak again until he was seated—McCoy having pulled his chair away from the table for him while Kirby took the crutches. The lame old man had elected to sit opposite Steele. "As to the cards, young feller, they are being delivered here direct from the makers. Sealed, of course. Will you allow Lee or Chuck to take your rifle? I understand you prefer to keep it close by you. But it is rather out of place in such surroundings. As you yourself pointed out, this is nothing like the south-side saloon where you last played cards. Just over there?"

He waved an arm to the side, to indicate where Chuck Kirby had placed his crutches on a table. Steele pursed his lips, was silent for a few moments, then nodded. McCoy started forward but Steele held up a staying hand. Then used the other one to set the Colt Hartford down lengthwise on the floor—and shove it by the stock to send it slithering across the floor. So that it came to rest beneath a table.

"And would you not be more comfortable without your hat and gloves, sir?"

"Is this draw or strip poker, feller?" Steele muttered, the irritation audible in his tone.

Ford, who was dressed in a black suit, blue vest and starched white shirt with a boot-lace necktie neatly knotted at the throat, grimaced at the remark and the manner in which it was spoken. His two men were immediately aware of thir boss's displeasure and made to step away from the sides of his chair and come around the table.

"Don't, you fools!" Ford rasped, transferring his anger away from the Virginian toward McCoy and Kirby. "Go and wait for the others."

Resenting Ford as much as Steele, the two men spun away from the table and moved out of the Illinois Room and into the lobby. Their footfalls, until they were muted by the carpet beyond the doorway, had a heavy, ill-tempered sound. When they had gone out of earshot, the emaciated old man said:

"Look, Steele. You've got the kind of background that fits you into a place like this. You could mix with people like me and Sam Sinclair and Lowell Banning and John Cline without being noticed. I never knew your father but I knew of him. Like me, he came from nothing and made something of himself. Started what could have become one of Virginia's finest families. I heard he got killed in the war and I don't know—"

"After the war," Steele corrected.

A thin hand waved in the air. "All right. But that doesn't matter here and now. Fact remains you had something fine and you either lost it or gave it up. You still have the background, though. Even if you are forced or you choose to spend most of your time in places like the Broken Promise Saloon in the company of men like Chuck Kirby—you still know how to behave in our present surroundings and how to mix with the kind of people who will be playing in this game. And I would ask you, please, to observe the conventions this evening."

"Make you a promise, feller," Steele said as voices sounded out in the lobby. Strange voices which entered the Illinois Room on a stream of cold air that smelled of the lake. As Ford looked hard at the Virginian, obviously suspecting that he would not enjoy what he was about to hear. "That each time I happen to look at you, I'll swallow my spit instead of messing up the floor with it. And that if my feelings about you get too much to control, I'll excuse myself from the table before I throw up."

The liver spots of age stood out more starkly than ever against the sudden paleness of Ford's slack skin. "If I were not a cripple, you slick tongued sonofabitch, I'd—"

"You'd still be an old man trying to be something you're not, feller," Steele cut in. "A whoremaster—and God knows what else—trying to buy respectability. And having to use muscleheaded gunmen to do your dirty work when you can't buy your way out of a mess."

Ford had had the presence of mind to keep his voice low when he began to castigate Steele. And the Virginian spoke softly, too. So that the pair of smiling men who came into the Illinois Room did not realize what kind of atmosphere they were puncturing with the noise of their entry.

"Evening to you, Justin!" the shorter, fatter, older man greeted. He was in his mid-fifties with a shiny red face under a thick matting of jet black hair.

"Foul weather," the second added as he shrugged out of his topcoat and shook it to scatter a spray of raindrops across the floor. "Only something as good as this evening promises to be would have brought me out on a night like it is."

He was in his early forties. Of medium height and build and with a square-shaped, weathered face. His hair was brown and he had a bushy mustache that was mottled with gray.

When both men had removed their topcoats they were seen to be wearing well-cut suits of much the same dark brown color. The older man wore a cravat, the younger one a necktie. Both of them wore rings and showed the curves of gold watchchains across the fronts of their vests.

"They don't know about that," Ford mouthed, his birdlike eyes pleading for the Virginian to understand.

"Won't find out from me," Steele allowed at a normal conversational level. But out of context the remark would mean nothing to the newcomers, and Ford vented a silent sigh and nodded his acknowledgement.

As the two men at the doorway handed their dripping coats and high hats to the scowling McCoy and approached the table in the center of the room, they continued to smile with their

164

mouths—while their eyes made a careful study of Adam Steele. And by the time it took them to reach their chairs, Justin Ford had brought himself completely under control. His coloring was back to normal, there was a smile on his thin face and when he spoke his tone of voice was a perfect match for his easygoing expression.

"Sam," he said to the older man. "This here is Mr. Adam Steele of the Virginia Steeles. Sam Sinclair. Lowell. Lowell Banning, this is Steele. He'll be playing for Ace. You did get my message about good old Ace not feeling up to a big game? And I guess neither of you have any reason to object to Mr. Steele playing for him?"

"None at all," Sinclair came back at once, having completed his survey of the Virginian. And now his smile touched the brown eyes as well as his mouth and the upward curve of every line on his face. "I always say a poker game's only as good as the players. And old Ace wouldn't pick just anybody to play for him."

"Virginia Steeles?" Banning posed, frowning and running the fingertips of his right hand along the bristles of his mustache. "I don't think I ever heard of that family?"

"We're in the plantation business," Ford supplied as the silence lengthened while Steele chose to remain silent. "Lowell here's in banking, young feller. And Sam's in railroads."

The Virginian had nodded to each man when Ford made the introductions. Now he did the same again. And it disconcerted the two newcomers that the man in hat and gloves and with a day's growth of beard did not speak. Then, just for a moment, Ford allowed his displeasure with Steele to show. But quickly repaired the damage to his attitude and opened a conversation about the rising costs of improvements to one of the city's stockyards: from which it emerged that Sinclair's railroad company and Ford's canning business were financing the project, with money loaned by Banning's bank.

From where he sat, impassive and silent, Steele was able to see out of the doorway and across the lobby to the desk where Ruddy stood, the clock on the wall above the clerk's head. When the hands on the face of this clock pointed to 7:55, the heat in the Illinois Room—which came from the stoves in the lobby and the flames of the kerosene lamps overhead—was again dispelled by a draft from the open front doors of the hotel.

Whereas there had been bright and cheerful chatter when Sinclair and Banning entered the Regency, the voices which sounded now were hard and harsh in their tones. The three men at the table with Steele curtailed their conversation and turned in their chairs to look toward the lobby doorway. As the obese Ace Cline waddled into view, dressed in a gray suit, black shirt and white cravat. He was scowling.

"Good evening, Ace," Ford greeted. "Something wrong?"

"I've brought a lady with me, Justin. Like to have her watch the game along with me."

"I know her, Mr. Ford!" Lee McCoy called from the lobby. "She's a Clark Street night-walker, sir."

"What makes you so much of a big shot you can put me down for being a woman who—"

"Let her in, Lee!" Ford intervened. "Since on this occasion Ace will not be taking a hand in the game, he may need some kind of distraction to keep his mind occupied. You gentlemen do not mind?"

He smiled as he looked at each of the other seated men in turn.

"Not at all, I'd say," Sam Sinclair replied eagerly. "A little feminine company is always to be welcomed, no matter what the occasion. I always feel."

"Your party, Justin," Banning added. "Allow in who you want. Just pleased to see that you've hired them same two private detectives to keep out unwanted guests."

The Virginian simply nodded.

"Got my men outside, too," John C. Cline said as the slatternly looking Laverne joined him in the doorway and took his arm, grinning her triumph back at the scowling McCoy. "Make double sure we won't be disturbed. If they can keep from beating up on each other."

The fat man glowered at the back of Ford's head as he escorted the over-dressed, heavily perfumed whore toward a table over at the side of the room.

"Something wrong?" Sinclair asked, disturbed by Cline's expression and tone of rancor.

Ford grimaced. "There was some misunderstanding between the detectives I hired . . ." His birdlike eyes looked briefly on Steele's level gaze and then shifted away. ". . . and Ace's associates. A matter of discovering exactly who it was that Ace had arranged to have play on his behalf. After all, with so much money on the table, it was in the best interest of everyone to—"

The atmosphere had just begun to warm up again, when the outer doors of the hotel were opened once more.

"Package for Mr. Ford," a youthful voice chirped.

"I'll take it," McCoy responded. "Here, now beat it."

"Gee, thanks, mister!"

The doors swung closed, as Laverne and Cline took their seats at the side table. And McCoy came into the Illinois Room, carrying a small brown paper-wrapped package.

"The cards, sir."

"Fine. Open the wrapping and put the package down here, Lee. Then get the money. Ace, aren't you going to sit beside the man you are staking?"

Cline, who was still ill-humored from learning about the rough treatment Craig Powell had received from Ford's men, eyed all the men at the well-lit table with equal bad grace. "If I could get that close to this kind of card game and not suffer stomach cramps, I wouldn't need Steele to play for me. Me and Laverne will be just fine over here."

McCoy went to the far end of the room and up on to the stage where he unlocked the door at the side and went through. Everyone except Steele who had his back to that part of the room, watched anxiously for the man with the tanned face to reappear. This included Chúck Kirby, Ruddy and Nancy La Salle who had all moved into positions out in the lobby where they could get an unobstructed view of what was happening in the Illinois Room.

When McCoy did emerge on to the stage he was unable to close the door behind him for he was laden with four packages. Wrapped in brown paper.

Steele did not see these until the man had delivered his burdens, lowering them on to the table to Ford's right and Banning's left, beside the unwrapped package of playing cards. Ford was smoking by then, but the foul smelling cloud of blue tobacco smoke from his cigar did not mask the fact that there were beads of sweat on his emaciated face. Banning and Sinclair also had warm, salty dampness on their brows and the sides of their jaws. And, although he could not see Ace Cline clearly, Steele guessed that the fat man was having a similar reaction to the prospect of seeing two million dollars in hard cash on the table.

Four wealthy men unable to completely control their emotions in the vicinity of more wealth: to which each had contributed a quarter share in the hope of winning the other three-quarters.

"All right, Lee, leave us," Ford said, more gravel voiced than usual. "You have your orders. Shoot to kill."

McCoy and Laverne in the room and the three people out in the lobby were also visibly affected by what they knew had to be in the brown paper-wrapped packages piled on the green baize covered table. And there was greed in their eyes, too. And envy. Even lust. But overlaying these powerful emotions was another of equal strength: the dejection of people who knew themselves to be indulging in futile wishful thinking.

"Right, gentlemen," Justin Ford said suddenly, turning back to the table after he had watched Lee McCoy go out of the Illinois Room and pull the double-doors closed behind him. He took out a silver watch from his vest pocket and pressed a button on the side of its case. "We will play until midnight, at which time my watch will sound an alarm. The name of the game is five-card-draw poker. Played according to Hoyle. No wild cards and no limit. Anything to open. First black jack deals. Any questions?"

As he spoke he distributed the money packages to the players, took one deck of cards from out of the unfastened wrapper and lowered the rest to the floor at his side.

Banning used a penknife to cut the twine which secured his package and then passed it to Ford who used it, gave it to Sinclair who in turn handed it to the Virginian when he was through with it. Talking seemed to ease Ford's nerves and his hands did not tremble as he unwrapped the paper. The banker and the railroadman were too eager and untidy, both of them tearing the wrappers.

"You always keep this kind of money in a back room, feller?" Steele asked, and despite being able to keep his hands steady, heard the quiver in his voice as he looked down at the neatly stacked bills which the unwrapping process had revealed.

The stacks were held by paper bands printed—like the blob of sealing wax on knots in the twine—with the name BANNING BANKING CORPORATION. All the bills were brand new and uncirculated. Thousand dollar and one hundred dollar notes. Too many stacks for the men to keep in front of them as they played.

"Right, gentlemen," Ford said again, after he and the others had relished the sight of the crisp new bills in their neat stacks. "Now that the letter of the condition of entry to this game has been met with, I suggest we divide our money into the folding kind and reserve."

He illustrated what he meant by dividing the pile of bills in front of him into two portions and transferring the larger part—still in the wrapping paper—to the floor at his left side. Then he pushed the unopened deck of cards into the center of the table.

"As a stranger among friends, you may break the seal and deal for dealer, Mr. Steele," the skinny old man invited. "And to reply to your question, no it is of course not my habit to keep so much ready cash close by me. But as soon as

171

it was agreed that this game should take place, it was arranged with Lowell's bank to have the necessary stake money brought here in total secrecy. All of us, of course, bank with the Banning Corporation. And have sufficient funds to cover what is in front of us."

"And plenty of back-up money, if needed," Ace Cline put in.

"Of course," Ford agreed, watching carefully along with Banning and Sinclair as Steele broke the seal, slid the virgin cards from the carton, scaled away the two jokers and then shuffled. They noticed that the scuffed and stained and torn gloves seemed to make no difference to his dexterity with the cards. "Although we will not risk bringing further cash here tonight. Once a man's stake is exhausted, markers will be used. Should he wish to continue, that is."

"We always play with money rather than chips, Mr. Steele," Sinclair added as the Virginian began to distribute the cards, face up around the table. "It is so much more pleasurable, we find. And our security has always been very well preserved by the detectives Justin hires and by Ace's fine men."

"You heard what I said to Lee," Ford supplemented. "If anyone so much as looks as if he might have designs on robbing us, he'll be wiped out."

"Your deal, feller," the Virginian said softly as the third card he turned over in front of Lowell Banning showed as the jack of spades.

As two gunshots exploded out in the lobby. The double doors burst open and McCoy and

Kirby came into the Illinois Room. At a staggering run, their scarred faces contorted by fear and pain.

"Table's turned," Steele rasped.

And turned the table.

Chapter Eleven

The Virginian was in the grip of a temper more furious than the one which had directed his actions in dealing with the hapless Chuck Kirby last night.

He had wanted badly to play in this big game. With men who had big money and could afford to lose it. For his appetite for easy money—and there was no easier money than that which a good player could take from bad players in a poker game—had been whetted by his experience at the Broken Promise Saloon.

For an opportunity to play in this game—against a man so lacking in self-confidence he tried to bribe Steele to cheat and two other men who this one claimed could be taken with ease—he had ridden with a lot of punches. He had allowed Cline and Powell and Coe to treat him like a fool—protecting him from the truth that the emaciated old man was fronting for Chicago criminals: which fact might scare off a run-of-the-mill card player. He had let McCoy get away, unpunished, with trying to have him murdered when Steele refused to accept money to stay away from the game. McCoy was obviously concerned that Ford was likely to show more than his poker hand if the cards went against him. And he had agreed to take part in Ford's charade of being an honest businessman for as long as the untarnished Sinclair and Banning were within earshot. Playing all these little games simply for the never-to-be-repeated chance of taking a hand in the biggest poker game ever. Without giving a thought to the consequences. Or suffering memories of Renita. But now that chance had been snatched away from him. And he recalled what another whore had said: *What does it matter? He will play anyhow.*

"Don't!" Ruddy shouted desperately.

"Oh, you bastard!" Nancy La Salle shrieked.

And both of them fired again the guns which were clenched so tightly in their fists. Big, long barrelled Colt .45s which had already blasted holes in the backs of McCoy and Kirby. Holes which spurted great blobs of crimson as the two men died on their feet and pitched forward to slam hard to the polished hardwood floor.

They had been shot at close range, by killers who from the way they fired again were not used to handling revolvers. The guns bucked and the bullets went high and wide.

As Laverne screamed in terror and Justin Ford roared in pain—the edge of the table overturned by Steele digging hard into his skinny thighs.

Then the old man started to go over backwards in his tipping chair, the move forced by the great weight of the table as it veered to a vertical attitude, tipping thousands of dollars to mix with the rest of the two million dollars on the floor.

Banning and Sinclair forced themselves backwards with deep-throated roars of fear. Then reached around to wrench their chairs out of the way and hurled themselves to the floor.

Steele let go of the table, raised his right leg and drew the knife from his boot sheath.

"We'll share!" Ruddy screamed at the top of his voice. "Steele, we'll—"

Ford's cry of agony and terror was curtailed as he slammed to the floor and the table fell, top down, across him. The green baize cover draped his unconscious form.

Just as the knife left Steele's gloved hand, which was stretched forward to the limit of the length of his arm. The spinning weapon powered with every ounce of the crouching Virginian's strength and rage.

The blade bit through Ruddy's jacket, vest, shirt, undershirt and flesh. And in no more than a second after leaving Steele's fingertips the finely honed metal was buried deep in the victim's chest. The slicing of the knife through his heart killed the man and the force with which the weapon was flung at him sent him staggering backwards. To crash against the doorframe and bounce off to fall face down on the floor.

"Oh!" Nancy wailed: drawing out the sound like a long and discordant note of eerie music. Then curtailed it as she raked her eyes away from the sprawled corpse of the man and swept her gaze back to the center of the room. Where the unmoving Justin Ford was hidden beneath the cover and the table, Banning and Sinclair were frozen by terror to the floor as they stared at the crazed woman with a gun in her fist: and Adam Steele made to race for the table under which he could see his rifle.

"None of you will have it!" she blurted suddenly, and took hold of the Colt in both hands to raise it high in front of her and aim along the top of the barrel. "If Ruddy and me ain't gonna have it, neither are you rich, snotnose, sonsofbitches!"

"No, don't!" Ace Cline shrieked. "That's two mill—"

As he lunged from his chair, tearing his gaze away from the woman to stare at the scattered bundle of bills around the overturned table, he collided with Steele. And with his massive bulk knocked the more slightly built man to the floor.

In going to the floor with a curse ripping from his lips, Steele saw what it was that had spurred the fat man into action. And, as Nancy squeezed the Colt trigger, recalled the derringer in his jacket pocket.

In the brand of rage which gripped him, there had been no room in his mind for such mundane memories as the time he had claimed Red Wilmot's tiny gun and put it away.

In the brand that had taken command of Nancy La Salle, the whore was able to hold the big gun rock steady. And send a bullet accurately up at the pulley from which the chandelier hung.

The fitting jerked an inch or so lower and swung.

"No, no, no!" Cline screamed as he leapt across the form of Sinclair and crouched down to start gathering up bundles of bills.

"Oh, sweet mother of God!" Sinclair rasped and struggled to belly out from under the dangerously poised group of kerosene lamps.

As Lowell Banning scrambled away from the center of danger in the opposite direction.

And Steele lunged the final few feet to get his hands to the Colt Hartford.

And another bullet from the whore's gun blasted the pulley out of its fixings—to bring the cluster of lamps crashing down to the floor. With a crash of metal, smash of glass and whoosh of small flames expanding to a great tongue of fire.

"I friggin' told you, you bastards!" Nancy screamed. "Die, die, die!"

The money was on fire. So was the cover draped over Justin Ford. The floor over a large area of the center of the Illinois Room. And the clothing and hair of the obese John C. Cline. Who died as one or perhaps both of the final two shots in the Colt .45 were blasted into the leaping flames by the ranting whore.

"Oh, Jesus, I'm gonna get outta here!" Laverne gasped, as she tore her gaze away from the holocaust in the center of the room and saw Steele rising to his feet beside her, a rifle angled across the front of his body.

"I wouldn't try," the Virginian advised her, and felt his anger turn suddenly from white hot to ice cold: the source of its vicious power shifting from his mind to the pit of his stomach.

And he raced forward, ignoring the rising figures of Sinclair and Banning. The back of one whore who had elected to ignore his warning. And the picture of remorse and dejection that was the other one standing between the corpses of McCoy and Kirby.

He held the rifle with one hand as he circled the area of leaping flames, reached down without breaking pace, grasped the wrist of Justin Ford's outflung arm and hauled the old man clear. From off the overturned chair and out from under the flaming cover and scorching table.

"Hold it!" a man yelled. And allowed no margin. For the shot rang out a split second after the order was shouted.

Steele came to a halt, released his hold on Ford's limp wrist and spun around, taking a double-handed grip on the Colt Hartford and levelling it from the hip.

Laverne had been racing for the door off the stage. The bullet from Niles Coe's gun took her low down in the back and sent her sprawling on to her belly. The momentum of her run and the impact of the bullet caused her to slide across the polished hardwood. She screamed her agony and fear until her head smacked against the front of the stage and knocked her out.

Or perhaps killed her.

Nobody cared enough to go and find out.

Yet.

As Steele and Sinclair and Banning, their backs to the blazing fire, looked at Powell and Coe and Nancy La Salle who stood just inside the threshold of the room.

After Coe had shot the only living thing in sight that was moving, neither he nor Powell seemed to know where to aim the guns they held.

"It seemed like a good idea," Nancy said dully against the crackle of flames. "They could all afford to lose that money without it hurtin'. It was just stuff to play games with to them. Money got from poor folks one way or another. We didn't make no fancy plans. Just figured to shoot folks and take the money. Folks that didn't deserve to go on livin' is how we figured it."

She was staring down at the empty gun in her hands as she spoke.

"Where's Cline?" Powell asked.

Nancy turned to look towards him.

Coe saw the gun for the first time. And fired instinctively. Even as Sinclair and Banning yelled in unison:

"No!"

It was a heart shot at close range. That sent the whore back half a pace and then dropped her into an untidy heap on the floor.

"That gun was empty!" Banning accused.

Steele started forward, closing in on the two men in the doorway. With his rifle aimed at a point midway between them.

"Cline?" Powell said, to the Virginian.

"Reckon you could say the fat's in the fire, feller."

Cline's men stared long and hard at the leaping flames which had now taken hold of the table and kerosene soaked area of the polished floor.

"Along with two million dollars," Sinclair growled, as Justin Ford groaned and rolled his head from side to side.

"Let's get out of here, Craig," Coe said suddenly.

"I'm with you, Niles," Powell answered. "You won't try to stop us, Steele?"

He nodded to the levelled Colt Hartford, acknowledging that he thought it could gun them down despite the fact that he and Coe continued to hold their revolvers—but not aimed.

"Grateful to you fellers for the chance you gave me. It wasn't your fault it turned out to be such a hot game in the wrong way."

The two men looked at each other, then swung around, thrusting their guns out of sight under their coats.

Steele followed at a more leisurely pace and out in the lobby angled across towards the desk behind which his gear was stowed. There was no sign of the liveried attendant out on the street beyond the doors which had closed behind Powell and Coe. He could sense someone

182

watching him from out of the darkness beyond the door below the stairs. And guess this would be the old-timer named Troy.

Footfalls rapped on the floor of the Illinois Room and Sinclair and Banning appeared in the doorway, pale-faced and dull-eyed with delayed shock.

"You should stay here to talk with the police, sir!" Sinclair said.

"What could I tell them you fellers couldn't?" Steele asked as he headed for the foot of the stairs, his gear carried easily over one shoulder while the rifle was canted to the other one: intent upon going out to the livery via the back stairway. "That they would want to hear?"

Banning cleared his throat. "That is hardly the . . . POINT!"*

---

* A full one to mark the end of this story. Adam Steele will be back again in the next book of the series.

183